TO WAIT FOR LOVE

Miss Delia Stockdale is engaged to Ambrose Staynford, Lord Coberley, but she does not love him. She suspects that he loves her sister, Katy; but Katy runs off to Gretna Green with the rakish Anthony Mayfield. In a cross-country chase after the couple, Delia is joined by Anthony's relative, Kester Mayfield and they have many misfortunes. Ambrose finds Katy, who has run away from Anthony, and all is resolved in this spirited Regency romance.

GILLIAN KAYE

TO WAIT FOR LOVE

Complete and Unabridged

LINFORD
Leicester

First published in Great Britain in 2005

First Linford Edition
published 2005

British Library CIP Data

Kaye, Gillian
    To wait for love.—Large print ed.—
Linford romance library
    1. Elopement—Fiction
    2. Love stories
    3. Large type books
    I. Title
    823.9'14 [F]

    ISBN 1–84617–106–7

Published by
F. A. Thorpe (Publishing)
Anstey, Leicestershire

Set by Words & Graphics Ltd.
Anstey, Leicestershire
Printed and bound in Great Britain by
T. J. International Ltd., Padstow, Cornwall

This book is printed on acid-free paper

1

When Delia heard the carriage at the front of the house, she was in her bedroom restringing a necklace of ivory beads which had broken as she was putting it round her neck that morning.

She laid the beads to one side but did not go down to the drawing-room to greet their visitor immediately. She knew it to be Lord Coberley and she also knew the reason for his visit.

Miss Delia Stockdale was dressed in a favourite sprig muslin of blue and white; it became her dark hair and blue eyes, but could not hide her tall sturdiness or the fact that she was no longer in the first flush of youth. For Delia was six-and-twenty and was neither dainty nor pretty; however a certain independence in her expression caused her friends and family to call her a handsome girl.

She was the eldest daughter of Sir James and Lady Stockdale of The Furlongs near Cheltenham in the county of Gloucestershire. She was also the eldest of their three children. Her brother, Andrew, was reading for the law at Oxford, and Katy, her sister, was just coming up to her eighteenth birthday.

That morning, Delia knew that Lord Coberley was calling to ask her to become his wife. He was their nearest neighbour at Ashleigh Court and a year previously had inherited the title on the death of his father. After the funeral, which the Stockdale family had attended, Ambrose Staynford, the new Viscount Coberley, had told Delia that it was time he entered the wedded state — his words had amused her. He would mourn his father for a year, he told her, then he would ask her to marry him.

So precisely a year later, Delia walked slowly down the stairs, knowing the purpose of Ambrose's visit. She had not made up her mind whether to accept him or not.

She knew him well, she liked him, but something made her hesitate. She had always regarded him as a favourite older brother and deep in her heart, she knew that despite her years, she yearned for something more than fondness in a marriage.

The Furlongs was an old house and spacious, the drawing-room being no exception. As Delia opened the door, it was to the sounds of laughter.

She saw immediately that her mother, sitting comfortably by a blazing fire, was smiling broadly. This did not surprise Delia for she knew Lady Stockdale to be very fond of Ambrose and that she had great hopes of a future alliance between the two families.

But what did surprise Delia was the sight of her young sister, Katy, in the middle of the room, laughing merrily at something Ambrose had said. Not only that, Katy was holding on to his hands and he seemed unusually animated.

In a sudden delight, Delia had the thought that perhaps Katy would do for Ambrose, then immediately her hopes were dashed as she remembered that her sister was only seventeen and had not yet made her come-out.

Ambrose, Lord Coberley, turned at that instant and Delia saw the smile he had directed at Katy turn to an expression of grave seriousness. Most described him as a handsome young man for he was tall and straight with immaculate brown hair and fine dark eyes, but as he was nearly thirty years of age and in her presence, usually ponderous, Delia was inclined to think of him as a dull stick. His moments of laughter with Katy as she had entered the room had surprised her.

'Delia,' he was saying now, 'I have waited a year for this day. Do fetch a pelisse and we will walk in the gardens. I will go and make my intentions known to Sir James and ask his permission to address you. I do not surprise you, my dear?'

Delia shook her head and remained serious though inwardly amused that Ambrose should go through the formality of asking her father's permission.

Her pelisse was a darker blue than her dress and her bonnet had matching ribbons and she stepped lightly at Ambrose's side. The gardens at The Furlongs were carefully tended and it being the early spring of the year 1812, the bright gold of daffodils was to be seen in every corner.

The sun shone, but the breeze was stiff, and Delia gave a little shiver. Ambrose turned to her.

'You are cold, Delia, I should not have brought you outside. Is there somewhere we can shelter?'

Delia smiled. 'The summer house, Ambrose, have you forgotten the summer house?'

She watched a smile of recollection lighten his eyes and thought he looked different. If only he was not so serious, she said to herself, I would not have the doubts that seem to be besetting me.

'Goodness gracious, Delia, to think I had forgotten the summer house. We used to play hide-and-seek around it and I seem to remember that we liked to sit there with our books if it was too wet to be outside.' He gave a laugh. 'And once I tried to kiss you and you would not let me. You were a prudish little thing. How easily one can forget one's childhood.'

Delia was amused at his response and felt hopeful. She might not love Ambrose in a romantic sense, but there was no denying that he was a good person. If she had a little ache in her heart which told her to wait for love, she dismissed it.

'They were happy times for us all, Ambrose. Do you remember when Katy fell into the lily pond and you waded in to help her out? Your breeches got a soaking and you were covered with weed.'

He laughed. 'I wasn't as wet as Katy,' he said. 'She was always up to some mischief or other.'

They had been walking through the shrubbery as they had been talking, and on the far side they reached a small, square wooden structure with no door and a wooden seat running all the way round the inside.

Delia sat down, but Ambrose seemed to take great care not to sit too close to her as he sat facing her on the opposite seat.

'Delia,' he said, slowly and deliberately. 'You know my reason for coming to The Furlongs on this day and you will be pleased to know that your father has given me permission to address you. We were talking of the times when we were children, but they are now in the past and I must look to the future. I come to you as Ambrose John Staynford, fourth Viscount Coberley, to request your hand in marriage.

'We are used to each other's ways and I am of the earnest opinion that it would be a very suitable match. You would not have to move very far from your parents and I know that you will honour the place that my mother, as dowager, will have at Ashleigh Court. In short, my dear Delia, I hold you in very high esteem and ask you to become my wife.'

As he stopped speaking and looked expectantly at her for a reply, Delia panicked. I cannot do it, I cannot. This is the Ambrose I have always known, surely he could have asked me in a more loving way. Am I wrong to expect love, she asked herself? Then she panicked again as she remembered that she was approaching thirty years and that this might be her last chance of matrimony. Or would I rather just be an aunt to Andrew and Katy's children, she thought rather hopelessly.

Even as she thought of Katy, she remembered the happy expression on her sister's face when she was greeting Ambrose earlier that morning. And the words slipped out.

'Thank you for your offer, Ambrose, but would you not prefer to marry Katy?'

To her astonishment, she saw a red flush come into his usually pale features. 'Katy? Katy?' he stammered. 'Of course Katy would not make a wife for me. What are you thinking of? The girl is only seventeen. It is true that I am very, very fond of Katy and that I would welcome her as a sister. But a wife?' He seemed to be asking himself a question. 'No, Katy is too young to become Lady Coberley, I think you will agree.'

Then Delia saw his expression change again. 'I am fond of you, too, Delia, you must know that. I am not a gentleman for flowery speeches, but I can assure you of my devotion if you were to become my wife. I am of the opinion that we could deal very happily together and I await your reply with eagerness.'

Even though he had once again lapsed into a stiff formality, Delia felt somewhat mollified. Ambrose had never been one for compliments and if his manner was punctilious, she knew that underneath that very formality, he was a likeable person.

I must think quickly, she was saying to herself, he is waiting for a reply. There are so many advantages, he is only a little older than myself, I have always known him to have an agreeable personality, I would be mistress of Ashleigh Court and not far from my own family . . . oh, have done with love and romance, she suddenly decided, and said the words Ambrose was waiting to hear.

'Thank you very much for your offer Ambrose, I am pleased to accept and I hope I will be a good wife to you.' Then she laughed at herself for being as stiff as he had been.

Ambrose leaned towards her from his seat and took her hand in his. 'I am delighted, Delia, may I kiss you?' Without waiting or a reply, he moved to sit at her side and touched her cheek with firm lips and with no hint of passion.

'Thank you,' said Delia again, accepting that kiss on the cheek was the limit of intimacy to which Ambrose would permit himself on this solemn occasion.

'We will go and tell your family,' he said as he helped her to her feet. 'And then, if you are agreeable, I would like to take you over to Ashleigh Court to see Mama. She knows of my mission this morning and she is anxiously awaiting your reply for she is very fond of you.'

Back in the drawing-room, all was gaiety and celebration. Sir James and Lady Stockdale were delighted to have their daughter make such a good marriage and were pleased to accept Ambrose as a future son-in-law.

It was Katy who was the most forthcoming. At almost eighteen years of age, she was fast becoming a beauty. She had the same dark hair and blue eyes as Delia, but where Delia was tall and felt herself to be ungainly, Katy was small-boned and succeeded in conveying a sense of delicate prettiness. The fine features of her face hid a mischievous wilfulness. She knew that she was a very pretty girl, but she was not vain and her manners were open and generous. Most of her acquaintances found her captivating.

Lord Coberley was one of these and as he and Delia entered the room and announced their engagement, a shriek came from Katy. She ran up to Delia and kissed her, then turned and took Ambrose by the hand.

'Ambrose,' she declared. 'I thought you would wait for me. You know I love you.'

For the second time in an hour, Delia saw a flush come into Ambrose's face and it made her wonder if, indeed, he did care for Katy. But he kissed the young girl sedately and did not show any embarrassment at her outrageous remark.

'Katy Stockdale, I love you, too, and you will be my dear sister. What could be nicer?' He managed to sound quite light-hearted and Delia was thankful that the sober mood of the summer house had passed.

Wine was brought in, congratulations resounded and it was a happy scene. Then Ambrose made his excuses.

'Lady Stockdale, I hope you will not mind if I take Delia off to Ashleigh Court. My dear mama will be waiting to hear the good news.'

'Of course you must go, Ambrose, and tell Lady Coberley how pleased we are at your happiness. We will be able to arrange an engagement party for you and Delia and I hope that she will come.'

In the curricle on the way to Ashleigh Court, Delia felt happier. She had Katy to thank for lifting the air of solemnity from Ambrose and she found that he chatted in an animated fashion on the short journey.

Delia had always admired Ashleigh Court and she knew it well. Ambrose was the only son of the Staynford family and his four sisters had been Delia's closest friends. They were now all married and living elsewhere in Gloucestershire and Somerset with

13

their husbands and numerous small children.

The dowager, Lady Coberley, was a tall and rather handsome woman of some fifty years of age and she greeted Delia with much affection.

'I know it must be good news for Ambrose has brought you to see me, and I am pleased that it is you, Delia. I did wonder if you would turn the dear boy down and he would come back with little Katy. Ambrose thinks the world of her and I would have been pleased to welcome her as his wife, but she is very young and can be such a naughty little scamp. But there, Ambrose is fond of you, too, indeed you have been as another sister to him along with our own and you have dignity, my dear girl.

'That is very important in the wife of a viscount as you will realise. I hope you will not mind sharing Ashleigh Court with me. It has always been the tradition for the dowager to have the west wing, so you need not fear that I

14

will be any trouble to you. You will be able to raise your family in comfort and send them to me when they get under your skirts as the saying goes. Come and give me a kiss for you will be my fifth daughter.'

Delia did as requested and was pleased to do so. She was used to Lady Coberley's ramblings and had never known a word of malice pass her lips.

Then her future mother-in-law continued as though there had been no interruption. 'Now, have you planned your wedding? I am out of black now so you are free to go ahead. It is nothing to do with me, but I always think that a summer wedding is nice and your gardens at The Furlongs are beautiful. And of course, we are very lucky in that both families attend Saint Mary's church in Prestbury.

'Decide upon a date and I will write and tell the girls. They will want to be here and their young families, too. Perhaps the older girls could be bridesmaids and of course, there is Katy to think of.

You must plan a very pretty gown for Katy, but, oh dear, I go on as though it is all my arranging and it is the bride's family who has the honour. Off you go now and talk it over between you.'

Outside the house, Ambrose and Delia paused on the steps of the porch.

'I will drive you up to Saint Mary's Hill before I take you home, Delia, and perhaps we can have a little talk about the wedding arrangements. Such a splendid view of the village from there and overlooking the church which seems quite appropriate, I expect you will agree.'

Delia could see that Ambrose was feeling pleased at his success of the morning, but she had many misgivings and it was to be the occasion of their first disagreement.

They sat quietly in the curricle. Delia's mind was full of Lady Coberley's words on the subject of their wedding and she was wondering how she was going to voice her objections to Ambrose.

'You are happy with a summer wedding, Delia?' he asked her.

She was silent, trying to gather her thoughts on the subject, she was certain of only one thing. She did not want the kind of fuss Lady Coberley had spoken of.

'Did you hear my question?' Ambrose spoke again and there was a slight edge to his voice.

'Yes, of course I heard you, Ambrose. I am trying to find a way of telling you politely that I do not agree with your mother.'

'You do not agree with Mama? Whatever can you mean? No-one ever disagrees with Mama.'

Delia sighed, she could sense that this was going to prove difficult.

'Ambrose, I am six-and-twenty and had expected to remain a spinster. You have kindly offered for me and I have accepted. But I do not want a stylish wedding with all your sisters and their families there. I would be happier if it could be just the two of us.'

He looked at her in astonishment. 'Surely you cannot mean that you want an elopement, Delia?'

Her reply came sharply. 'Of course I do not mean an elopement. Whatever are you thinking of? Do I look the kind of young lady who would elope?'

Ambrose was blunt. 'No, if you were that frivolous, I would never have asked you to marry me.'

Delia looked up at him. 'Wouldn't you, Ambrose?' She had the sudden outrageous feeling that she would like to be engaged to the sort of young gentlemen who would have whisked her off and eloped with her. She tried to stifle her feelings and waited for his reply.

'No, of course I would not. What are you talking about, Delia? You had better tell me what is in your mind so that I will know what to do for the best. You do wish to marry me?'

'Yes, I think so,' she replied and it was miserably spoken.

'And what is that supposed to mean? Are you having second thoughts? What has happened to overset your feelings?'

'I am sorry, Ambrose, I expect that all young ladies have doubts when it comes to talking of arranging a big wedding ceremony as your mama has done. I don't want to quarrel about it. I would simply like a quiet affair.'

'A quiet affair? But our marriage will be a great local occasion, the Stockdales and the Staynfords.'

'I dare say it is, but I do not want the kind of fuss your mother suggested.' Delia was adamant.

'You are seeking a quarrel with me, Delia, in spite of what you said. How is it possible to leave out my sisters and their children? I will not do it.'

Delia looked at him. So he can be obstinate, she thought, but I am determined to have my way.

'Then I will cry off before we go any further,' she snapped.

'Cry off?' he echoed. 'Whatever are you talking about?'

'If we think differently about the style of wedding we are going to have, then we will think differently about other

19

things, too. I do not think we are suited in spite of the fact that we have known each other all our lives.' Delia felt both unhappy and uncertain.

To her surprise, Ambrose put his arm around her shoulders. It was a rare gesture for him and she experienced some comfort.

'I'm beginning to understand,' he said, suddenly quiet. 'Mama has frightened you with her talk of all my sisters coming and bringing their vast broods, I might have known it. It is a big day to see her only son married. Is that what it is all about?'

She nodded. 'I have no wish to offend your mother right at the start, but I would prefer to have a simple ceremony at Saint Mary's with just you and your mama, and my parents, and Katy, of course.'

'Katy will want to be a bridesmaid.'

'Yes, I know, but I do not want a bridesmaid,' she replied hastily.

'She would make a very pretty one.'

Again, Delia looked up at him, but

she could not read his expression. It seemed to her to be a rather brooding faraway look.

'You think Katy is pretty?' she asked and wondered what his reply would be. She was unprepared for his response to her light-hearted question.

'I think Katy is the loveliest girl I have ever seen.'

The intensity of his reply startled her, and her words burst from her.

'Then marry Katy. I have said that once today already.'

She had never seen Ambrose angry before. His face was red, his hands were clenched on the reins. He seemed to find it difficult to speak.

'Delia Stockdale, I have told you why it is you I wish to marry. I might be very fond of Katy and I suppose I am allowed to think her as beautiful, but it is you I have chosen to be my wife. If you think that is unreasonable then I will allow you to cry off but please think carefully before you reply.'

He would have chosen Katy if she

had been a little older she was thinking. If I marry Ambrose I will have to be prepared to be second best.

'Ambrose, I am sorry if I am being difficult, it is a big moment in a young lady's life. Let us talk of the wedding and if we can agree on a quiet affair, perhaps I will see things more clearly. What about a summer wedding as your mama suggested? It is Katy's eighteenth birthday next month and she is making her come-out. Mama has arranged a ball at the Assembly Rooms in Cheltenham. We could plan a day sometime after that.'

He nodded. 'Yes of course, I did know that it was Katy's birthday soon and she told me about her ball. If that is in May, shall we give your mama time to recover and plan our wedding for July?'

Delia sighed with relief. July seemed a long way off, and by that time, she might have become accustomed to the fact that she was to marry Ambrose Staynford, Viscount Coberley for convenience and not for love.

2

Ambrose drove Delia back to The Furlongs, and Delia's mother seemed delighted with the idea of a July wedding. She bowed gracefully to Delia's wishes for it to be a quiet affair as she had not looked forward to entertaining the four Staynford girls, as she called them. She knew that they had twenty children between them ranging in age from one to eleven years.

Delia felt tired after the events of the day and that evening went up to her bedroom as soon as they had taken their tea. Katy joined her a little later, seemingly keen to have a private talk about the day's affairs.

The two girls had adjoining bedrooms and it was a habit of Katy's to spend the last half-hour of the day sitting on Delia's bed where she enjoyed a coze with her sister.

Delia had always accepted that Katy was the prettier of the two of them and had never begrudged her sister her looks. That evening, after hearing Ambrose's rather surprising words, she looked at Katy afresh.

In many ways, the two sisters were alike. The one much taller than the other, but both with the same dark hair and blue eyes. There the likeness ended. Delia was a serious girl, not plain, but usually pensive. She was even-tempered and rarely flew into a freak as Katy was wont to do.

Katy was slimmer than Delia and seemed almost fragile in appearance. In a face which was classically pretty, it was her eyes which the onlooker would always notice. The brightest blue and usually smiling, often with mischief for she had a lively sense of humour. For all her look of frailty, she was strong-willed and liked her own way. She was much loved in her family.

That night, she was eager to hear from Delia the details of the day's romance which had not been mentioned in front of their mother and father.

In spite of feeling tired, Delia was glad to see Katy, for she was despondent and not at all sure that she had made the right decision in respect of a marriage to Ambrose. She was already in bed when Katy appeared, sitting against her pillows, a book, as yet unopened, in her hand.

Katy sat herself on the end of the bed. 'Delia, are you excited?' she asked breathlessly. 'Do you love Ambrose? I know that you told Mama that you do not want a grand ceremony, but can I be a bridesmaid? I could wear my ball dress, it is made already.'

But Delia was impatient. 'Oh, do stop talking about it, Katy. I almost wish that I had never agreed to a marriage to Ambrose.'

'Never agreed? Whatever do you mean. I always thought you meant to marry him.' Katy was agog.

'It is not an easy decision when it is

for the rest of your life, Katy.'

'Well, if you don't want to marry him then I will. I would be Lady Coberley.'

'Katy!' Delia was shocked.

'Why not?' returned her irrepressible sister. 'Ambrose likes me, he always has done. I think he loves me more than he loves you, but you are the eldest and if I married him you would be left on the shelf.'

Delia sat up very straight. 'Katy, I think I am going to lose my temper with you.'

Katy put out a hand. 'I am sorry, Dee,' she said penitently and using the old pet name. 'I thought it would all be so romantic and it is not at all if you are not sure if you love Ambrose or not. He is quite good-looking, you know, and he is a viscount after all.'

Delia sighed. 'I am afraid that being a good-looking viscount stands for very little if one's heart is not engaged.'

'You don't love him at all,' announced Katy. 'I would only marry the man whom I truly loved, except for Ambrose, that is, he is different. Ambrose is rather special. But I am waiting for a dashing young hero to come along and sweep me off my feet, I will have no doubts, as you have.'

Delia laughed then. However cross her younger sister might make her, she always ended up by being amused by her.

'Perhaps you will meet him at your come-out ball, Katy. I am sure that the Assembly Rooms are a good place for romance. Go along now and allow me to read a few pages before I go to sleep. Perhaps the exploits of Isabella in Castle Rackrent will help me take my mind off Lord Coberley.'

* * *

It so happened that Miss Katy Stockdale did meet the hero of her dreams at her come-out ball.

A month had passed and in that time, Delia had become resigned to her engagement to Lord Coberley. The days passed pleasantly enough for she and Ambrose had for many years been in the habit of riding out together. Katy was no horsewoman and preferred a walk into the village where her greatest friend was Patience Hewitt, the youngest daughter of the rectory family.

When their brother, Andrew, came down from Oxford, he was always willing to accompany Katy on her walk as he was rather taken with Patience.

The day of the come-out ball arrived amid tears and tantrums because Katy's ball gown was too short. Delia could not believe that her sister had grown in the two months since the gown was made. She pacified her excited sister by sitting all the morning adding a small flounce of white lace to the hem of the underskirt and Katy was happy once more.

She had refused to appear all in white as was the custom and her underskirt was covered with a fine gauze of pale primrose, flecked with gold. The tight bodice was not daringly low as was the fashion, but more befitting a slim young girl of Katy's age. Delia had to admit that Katy looked lovely indeed. Her dark hair was piled high with escaping ringlets and fastened with small flowers the colour of her gown.

The Assembly Rooms in Cheltenham were a glittering affair on the night of Katy's ball. Chandeliers hung from the ceiling and the sconces around the walls were brilliant with many candles.

Ambrose and the dowager, Lady Coberley, joined the Stockdale party, Ambrose looking imposing in dark blue with white pantaloons and a silver grey waistcoat. Andrew, in younger fashion, sported an elaborate cravat and a vivid gold and white striped waistcoat. He had promised to lead Katy out for her first dance.

It was as Katy came back to their seats after the dance that the inevitable happened. Katy looked not only lovely, she looked happy, her blue eyes shining, her pretty mouth curved in many smiles and laughter.

She was talking to Ambrose and trying to persuade him to join the quadrille, when Delia who was watching them both, saw Katy go very still. She was staring across the room and she stopped speaking in the middle of a sentence, clutching at Ambrose's arm.

'Ambrose, who is that?'

He looked down at her. 'Whom do you mean, Katy? I know most people here.'

Delia glanced in the same direction as Katy and saw immediately the object of her sister's attention. A young gentleman standing with a party of guests who seemed to be his brothers and sisters, possibly his cousins.

Katy tugged at Ambrose's arm. 'On the other side of the room, Ambrose, a tall, fair young gentleman, he is wearing yellow pantaloons and a purple coat, high shirt points, you cannot mistake him.'

'Good God, Katy, the fellow's a curst dandy.'

'You must know who he is,' Katy sighed.

'Well, I don't.' Ambrose snapped uncharacteristically. 'And if I did, I would not introduce him to you. Seems to me he is with the Curtis set. Not a good crowd, Katy.'

But Katy was not satisfied and turned to her brother. 'Andrew, do you know who that young gentleman is? He is very handsome, long fair hair, looking in this direction.'

Andrew, gallantly trying to help his sister, looked across the room and gave an exclamation.

'Well, if it ain't Mayfield. Was at Eton with him. Yes, this is his father, Sir John Mayfield, and the girls must be his sisters. Might have a bit of sport here, Katy, if he is interested in you. Bit of a rogue, Mayfield, but can't imagine what he's doing here. Thought he was in disgrace over some gaming venture and he was being sent into the Navy. I'll introduce him willingly, Katy, though I warn you that he's a scoundrel in spite of looking like a young Adonis. Stay there.'

Andrew walked across to the other side of the Assembly Rooms and touched the young gentleman on the arm. He was greeted with a bow and a smile and Mr Anthony Mayfield willingly left his party to walk with Andrew towards Katy.

'Katy,' Andrew said, 'this is Anthony Mayfield, my younger sister, Katy, Mayfield. Thought you'd like to meet her; pretty girl, ain't she? Oh, and my mother and father, Sir James and Lady Stockdale.'

The young Mr Mayfield made his bow to the ladies and shook hands with Sir James.

'Think you might know my father, sir, the Mayfields of Pelham Grange on the other side of Winchcombe. I had forgotten that Andrew lived so near.'

Sir James nodded pleasantly. 'Yes, we did send an invitation, I am very pleased that you could come. Nice to have young people about us.'

Katy heard none of this. She was staring at the handsome Anthony.

'I am enchanted to meet you, Miss Stockdale,' he was saying. 'I cannot call you Miss Stockdale, might I have your permission to call you Katy? I think Andrew said that was your name. Katy, did you know that you are the most beautiful young lady here?'

'I consider myself passably good-looking, Mr Mayfield,' Katy replied and her voice was hushed with awe.

'Now don't come over bashful with me for I can tell that you are no prim little miss. And for Heaven's sake, do call me Anthony, I know we are going to be friends, your eyes said so the moment I crossed the room to greet you. It was a piece of good fortune that I was at school with your brother, he was almost very studious. Quite the opposite to myself, I am bound to tell you. I could not wait to go up to the capital and let myself loose.

'A fine couple of years I had until I had a run of bad luck at the tables and had to come home on a repairing lease. And to think it has brought me to you, I can hardly call that bad luck, can I? Come and join me in the quadrille.'

'I was trying to persuade Lord Coberley to dance,' Katy replied.

'He can dance with your sister, I believe I saw an announcement of their engagement in *The Times*.'

Katy nodded. 'Yes, Ambrose and Delia are engaged and hope to be married in July. I am very pleased about it for I have always loved Ambrose, admired him, that is.'

The handsome young man took her by the arm. 'Now you can admire me. I would like that and I will be the proudest gentleman in the room to have you as my partner.'

'I believe you like to flatter, sir,' said an already adoring Katy.

Delia had been watching the pair and she could not feel pleased. It was obviously apparent that young Mayfield was used to sophisticated London ways and that his flattery was making an easy conquest of Katy. She turned to Ambrose expecting to take his arm and be led on to the floor.

'No, Delia, if you do not mind, I will not dance the quadrille. What do you think of Katy's beau? Handsome is he not? They make a striking pair. I hope Katy does not lose her heart to him, though the Mayfields are a respectable family.'

'You know them, Ambrose?'

'I do not know them personally, but I recall that my father was once acquainted with Sir John Mayfield. I believe that they live near Winchcombe, you will probably find young Mayfield riding over to visit Katy. You must make sure that she is chaperoned, Delia.'

Watching the young couple and seeing their delight when they met in the set, Delia decided that her task would not be easy. It was obvious that Katy had fallen in love with the young man on sight and that he was about to carry on an easy flirtation.

★ ★ ★

It was inevitable, after the success of her come-out ball, that Katy would pour her heart out to Delia when it came to their bedtime.

Looking at her sister sitting at the bottom of the bed in a white night-gown, Delia thought that Katy looked more beautiful than ever and that it was a good thing that Anthony Mayfield could not see the young girl, in pure white, her dark hair tumbling in curls about her shoulders.

'Well, Katy, did you enjoy your come-out ball?' Delia asked, knowing that she was opening floodgates of confidences.

'Oh, Delia,' Katy sighed. 'Did you ever see such a handsome young gentleman as Anthony — he did ask me especially to call him Anthony. Such beautiful fair hair, so unusual in a gentleman and worn at such a flattering length. We decided that we had the same blue eyes, is that not romantic?

'He is to come in his curricle every day to see me and he will take me for drives as I do not like to ride. He did not mind that at all, he is all consideration. I have never felt so happy. To think that I should meet Anthony on the very evening of my come-out . . . did you say something, Delia?'

Delia's mind was racing. It will not do, she was telling herself, it will not do. He might be as handsome as Katy says, I do not deny him that, but I can see that he is going to break her heart. He is a young gentleman of no substance and of dubious reputation from what I heard from Andrew.

It seems he was sent from Eton because of a scandal with one of the maids who was found to be expecting his child. He did not even deny it, Andrew said, and went off to London to spend two years in and out of gambling hells. But I must not blacken his character in Katy's eyes, she is so happy though I do believe that Andrew regretted introducing them to each other when he saw what was happening. However, Anthony is home with his family again now which does bode well. I will be careful what I say, Delia thought to herself.

'I was going to say, Katy, that Anthony Mayfield is very young, so please do not raise your expectations too high. I doubt he is in a position to support a wife.'

Katy flew up into the boughs. 'As if I should think of such a thing, we have only just met. He may grow tired of me and then he is destined for the Navy for he told me so. I do not think of marriage, Delia, but it is my very first romance and it is very exciting. It is more exciting than loving Ambrose.'

Delia frowned heavily. 'Whatever are you saying, Katy?'

'I told you before how I was very fond of Ambrose, I would have accepted him if he had offered for me and not for you. I did tell you, Delia. I did think I loved Ambrose until I met

Anthony this evening, that is strange, both have names beginning with A, I wonder if it means anything. Did you say something, Delia?'

'No, I yawned, I am very tired.' Delia was also losing patience with her flibbertigibbet of a sister. 'I am pleased that your ball was such a success, Katy, now I think we had better settle down and get some sleep. It is two o'clock in the morning.'

* * *

Next morning, Delia was to find Katy in a state of nervous anticipation as she wondered if Anthony Mayfield would keep his promise and come to see her.

Lady Stockdale seemed to have no objection to a visit from the young gentleman. It pleased her to know that the ball had been a success and that Katy was happy. She knew nothing of Anthony's chequered history.

By eleven o'clock, Delia had a nervous Katy on her hands. She knew that Ambrose would not be coming that morning as he had business to attend to in Cheltenham. Delia felt that he would have known how to deal with an over-excited eighteen-year-old.

'He is not going to come, Dee, I know he is not going to come. Do all young gentlemen say they are going to do something and then forget all about it?'

'I don't know, Katy, Ambrose certainly always keeps a promise if he makes one. I cannot speak for Anthony Mayfield.'

'He was so charming to me, he whispered things which would put you to the blush if I told you . . .'

Delia interrupted quickly, 'Katy, I trust that you know how to behave with a young gentleman.'

'Oh, it was nothing improper, I can assure you. Just very personal and I had only just met him . . . what was that?' She broke off and her voice rose sharply. 'I think I heard wheels on the gravel outside.'

She rushed to the window and her voice rose even higher. 'It is Anthony, he is getting down from his curricle. Oh, he has come just as he said he would.'

When the maid announced him, Delia was surprised at his appearance after the dandy-set look of the evening before. He was quite sober in fawn pantaloons and a deep navy coat which fitted his figure exquisitely. He is out to impress, thought Delia, as she watched the two of them meet.

'Katy, good morning and good-day to you, Miss Stockdale.'

He made a bow and Delia could understand why Katy was so charmed. 'No, please call me Delia,' she replied. 'And as I have heard nothing but your name since we returned from the Assembly Rooms, I can only call you Anthony.'

'Delia,' Katy shrieked. 'You put me to shame for I have been very modest in the way I have spoken of Anthony.'

He took her hands and Delia saw the

lovely flush which passed over her sister's face.

'Now, young lady, would you like a drive in the curricle with me? It is a fine morning so please do not say no. Fetch a pelisse and bonnet for I will not take no for an answer. I will talk to your sister, but please do not take too long as the morning is half over already. I've no doubt that you were expecting me at the crack of dawn, but I was a lazybones after the delightful exertions at your ball.'

Katy disappeared and the young man turned to Delia. 'I can see that your mama is not here, will she approve of Katy coming for a drive with me? I can assure you that your sister will come to no harm.'

Delia was inclined to be impressed by his politeness and consideration.

'Mama is somewhere in the garden cutting flowers for the house. It is a favourite pastime of hers and she loves to arrange them, you will see that we are almost like a flower garden in the house!'

They both looked at the various silver and porcelain vases and bowls filled with pretty arrangements.

Anthony smiled. 'It is nothing out of the ordinary to me, for my mama has the same passion at Pelham Grange, that is our home near Winchcombe. I was pleased to find last night that the beautiful young lady who had caught my attention lived so near. Katy's looks are exceptional, don't you think?'

Delia answered him evenly. 'Katy has always been the pretty one and as she grows older and has a little more poise, then I think she will become a beauty. But please don't tell her so, we are trying to prevent her from becoming too vain of her looks.'

'I will tell her about the days when I was at school with Andrew. Do you know, I had quite forgotten that he lived in this part of the world. It was a pleasure to meet with him again last night. What does he intend to do when he finishes at Oxford?'

'He is reading for the law and I have

no doubt that he will end up becoming a London barrister, he is the clever one of the three of us . . . ' Delia broke off as Katy returned to the room wearing a blue pelisse and a straw bonnet trimmed with daisies.

Anthony exclaimed with a note of admiration in his voice. 'Ah, here is my little companion. You look charming, Katy, you should always wear blue, though I did admire your cream and white gown of last night. It was very suitable.' He turned to Delia. 'I will take Katy in the direction of Leck-hampton, there arc fine views to be had from the top of the hill there.'

Delia watched Anthony help a very happy Katy to climb on to the curricle and they were off, the horses taking a very sedate pace down the drive of The Furlongs.

3

During the next few weeks, the Mayfield curricle was to be seen at the Stockdale's front door almost every day. Neither Delia or her mother could fault Anthony's behaviour and as Katy was radiantly happy, they felt satisfied with the growing romance.

Unknown to them, Sir James had been making discreet enquiries about the young gentleman. While he had a marked respect for the Mayfield family, he soon found that there were tales circulating about the past misdeeds of young Anthony. He said nothing, but watched developments carefully.

It was just two weeks after the come-out ball that Anthony asked Katy to marry him. Their favourite trip out of Prestbury was to take a narrow lane which rose to the edge of Cleeve Common. Once there, they were content to sit close to one another in the curricle and to enjoy a view which on a fine, clear day seemed to stretch as far as the Malvern Hills. There seemed to be many such days that spring.

'I shall soon be saying goodbye to these parts,' said Anthony very suddenly on one of these occasions.

Katy, knowing that she had fallen in love with the young gentleman, went pale. 'What do you mean, Anthony?'

'It was intended that I went into the Navy, but my father has arranged a post for me as secretary to Lord Shurlock in Gloucester. He insists upon me carrying out his wishes or my allowance will be stopped. He is very generous, you know.'

Katy was pale with agitation. 'Does it mean you will go away and that we will not be able to see one another?'

'I am not sure,' he answered her and the reply was enigmatic. 'It all depends on your wishes, Katy.'

'But what have I to do with your going to Gloucester to live? All I understand about it is that we shall be parted.'

'We need not be parted if we were to marry,' he said as calmly as though he was asking her to admire the view.

'Anthony?'

One of his arms went round her shoulders and letting go of the reins, he took her hands in his. 'Katy, I love you, you must know that, and I believe that you love me. Tell me you love me.'

Katy met his eyes honestly and adoringly. 'I cannot deny it. I do love you, Anthony. I will do whatever you say and if we can be married then it would be the most splendid thing that had ever happened to me.'

'Will you allow me to kiss you, Katy?'

'Oh, Anthony . . . ' and her words were stopped by his lips on hers in a long kiss which was Katy's first.

They arranged between them that Anthony would see Katy's father later that day, then they decided that they would just have time to call the banns and to be married before Anthony took up his post in Gloucester. Katy was all smiles.

But once back at The Furlongs, the smiles ceased. Anthony sought an interview with Sir James and it did not go well.

The young gentleman was at his politest, but it did not impress Sir James Stockdale.

They faced each other across Sir James' desk in the library.

'Sir James, you will know that I have become very attached to Katy these last few weeks, I love her dearly. It is my most earnest wish to marry her and I seek your permission to address her. I have a very good allowance from my father and in a few weeks time, I start as secretary to Lord Shurlock in Gloucester; my father was influential in obtaining the post for me and there is a small house for my use.

'I would like to marry Katy before I take up my duties so that we can begin our married life in Gloucester and she would not be too far from you and her mother. Katy knows that I love her and I sincerely believe that she returns my affection. I trust I have your permission.'

Sir James had listened to this impassively and Anthony was not prepared for the viciousness of his reply.

'Young man,' he said sternly. 'I have every respect for your father, Sir John Mayfield and also for your mother who is known to my wife. I believe that they lived near each other when they were young girls. There my respect ends. How two such good people could have bred and nurtured such a loose-living and misguided youth as yourself is beyond my comprehension. I know everything about your disgraceful behaviour at Eton and your taking up with an element of London society known for its dissipation and wild life. I think that is where your father must have made his mistake.

'The pleasures and vices of London life do not bear comparison to the strict discipline of learning at Oxford and Cambridge. I know this from observing my own son, Andrew, who manages to combine a lively social life with an academic career quite successfully.

'I would never allow a daughter of mine to marry a gentleman of such profligate and licentious ways as yours. You may leave me and you may leave the house. I will speak to Katy. I do not even offer the courtesy of bidding you good day.'

Seconds later found a shaken Anthony standing in the entrance hall of The Furlongs where he found a starry-eyed Katy waiting for him.

Her smile faded when she saw his face. 'What is it, Anthony? Papa?'

They spoke in hushed voices and in their distress, neither noticed that Delia was about to come down the stairs and that she paused as she saw them, and noticed that they were upset about something.

'Katy, I will have to think. Your father has refused me and he will want to see you . . . I must go, he has forbidden me the house. Will you meet me this evening? I will be in the shrubbery at about nine o'clock, please say that you will be there.'

'Yes, yes, of course I will,' Katy whispered. 'Go quickly.'

Just as the door closed, Sir James appeared, he was frowning heavily. 'Go into the drawing-room, Katy and make sure that your mother is there, and Delia . . . ah, there you are,' he said to his eldest daughter as she continued down the stairs. 'I do not suppose that Andrew is in.'

By the time they were all gathered in the drawing-room, Katy had tears in her eyes, and she was clinging to Delia.

'Lady Stockdale, Delia, Katy . . . ' started Sir James very stiffly. 'I want you all to know that Mr Anthony Mayfield has made an offer for Katy and that I have turned him down. I regret to say that I have discovered him to be a young gentleman of wild and rakish habits and that he has disgraced the good name of Mayfield at the London gaming tables.

'If you think you have fallen in love with him, Katy, then all I can say is that it happened very quickly and that you can fall out of love with him just as quickly. I will never give my permission to a marriage between you and Anthony Mayfield, and I do not wish to hear his name mentioned again. That is all. Lady Stockdale, you had better ask for some tea to be brought.'

Delia held the sobbing Katy and met her mother's eyes. Lady Stockdale was full of sorrow and understanding. She had liked Anthony.

'I will go up to my room,' Katy said, her face half buried in Delia's shoulder.

'No, you won't,' her sister replied briskly. 'You will stop crying and walk in the garden with me.'

Outside the house, Katy did as she was told and stopped herself from crying by thinking of the meeting she was to have with Anthony that evening. He will not let me down, she was thinking. Perhaps he will elope with me.

At her side, Delia spoke with sense. 'Cheer up, Katy, you are only eighteen, you are sure to meet a more eligible gentleman before very much longer.'

'There isn't anyone else, only Ambrose.'

Delia was startled. 'But Ambrose is going to marry me.'

'I know, I do know. But I am sure he would have chosen me if I had been older, I have said so before. Oh, I admire him so much that I think I really do love him. Oh, it is not the same as I feel for Anthony, it is something quite different. You are my dear sister, Delia, but I am sure you cannot understand for you have never been in love even though you have agreed to marry Ambrose.'

Whatever shall I do with her, Delia thought, I had better try to change the subject quickly. But Katy would only talk about her life being ruined and Delia gave up any more attempts and took her sister back into the house.

When Andrew came home, he tried

to reason with his sister, but to no avail. Anthony might have behaved badly in the past, she told her brother, but he was different now and she loved him.

Delia thought long and hard that day. She had a strong feeling that Anthony would try to persuade Katy to elope with him. By now, she did know of his wild life in London and she imagined that although Anthony might succeed in coaxing Katy to run off with him, she doubted that the young man intended marriage.

During the evening, with Lady Stockdale, Delia and Katy busy at their needlework in the drawing-room, Sir James as usual in the library and Andrew busy preparing for his return to Oxford after the Easter break, it soon became apparent that Katy was in a fidget.

Delia watched her. She would get up and look out of the window, then return to her stitches which were very half-heartedly made, then unpicked and worked again. All the time, she was anxiously glancing at the clock on the mantelpiece.

Soon after half-past eight, Katy got up and walked towards the door, turning back to Lady Stockdale.

'Mama, I am feeling very warm and in the need for air, the evening is very close, don't you think? I am going to take a turn in the garden.'

'Certainly, my dear,' Lady Stockdale replied. 'But do take your Norwich shawl with you in case it is cooler than you think when you get outside. Do you wish Delia to accompany you?'

'No, no,' Katy said hastily, too hastily, Delia thought. 'I will just have a walk round the rose garden.'

She left the room and Delia said nothing, but went to the pianoforte and played some airs of Handel for a few minutes. All the time, her mind was on Katy's movements, but in the end she had no need for any subterfuge.

'Delia,' Lady Stockdale said. 'Katy has not returned. Do you think you should go after her? Perhaps she was not feeling well with the closeness of the evening and I know she is still upset over this business with young Mayfield. She may be glad to talk to you quietly on your own, you will know what to say as you are very sensible and not as easily upset as dear Katy.'

Delia rose and walked to the window. 'I cannot see her, Mama, but I will do as you say. Do not worry if we are gone a little while. I expect Katy will want to weep on my shoulder.'

'Yes, of course, my dear,' Lady Stockdale said. 'I can understand how Katy feels for she is very like me. It will be hard for you to believe, but when I was Katy's age, I fell in love with more than one unsuitable young gentleman! But then I met your dear father and my life was changed.'

Delia smiled affectionately at her mother and left the room to slip upstairs for a shawl. Within minutes, she was out of the front door and creeping round to the back of the house so that she could approach the shrubbery from the opposite direction to Katy and Anthony.

It was not difficult to hide in the shrubbery. The various shrubs had been planted too close together and although they were kept carefully clipped by the Stockdales' gardener, there was very little space between them.

Delia could see no sign of Katy and guessed that she was sitting in the summer house waiting for Anthony. That young gentleman was not to be seen, either, and Delia crept up behind the summer house and positioned herself where she could hear anything that was being said, but could not be seen.

There was nowhere to sit and she resigned herself to a long wait. It was a warm, close evening as Katy and her mother had said, it was also getting dark. She did not imagine that it would be more than a few minutes before Anthony arrived. If he did come, she added to herself.

She was right though, and she very

soon heard a loud whisper.

'Katy, are you there?'

'Oh, Anthony.'

Delia had not heard him approach and imagined that he must have left his curricle by the gatehouse and found one of Joe Passey's lads to hold the horses' heads — Joe Passey was the Stockdales' coachman.

She was alert to every sound and pleased to find that she could hear their voices quite clearly. What she heard appalled her, but somehow gave her no surprise.

'Katy, let me give you a kiss, then I will tell you what I have planned. You have not changed your mind? Do you love me?'

'Oh, I do, Anthony, I really do,' came the fervent reply.

'Good, now listen to what I have to say . . . '

'Is it an elopement?'

A quiet chuckle came from Mr Mayfield. 'Yes, it is. Listen carefully. We will have to drive to Gretna Green . . . '

'To Gretna Green? Oh, I cannot believe it. Do you think I will dare to come with you?'

'You will if you love me as I love you. I will kiss you again to show you how much I love you.'

There was a silence, and outside in the dusk, Delia clenched her fists to stop herself rushing to stop her sister. She must listen carefully to the arrangements they were about to make so that she would know how to stop them. If she interrupted them now, she knew Katy well enough to be aware that her sister would simply find another way to get what she wanted.

Then came Anthony's voice, and quite clearly this time. 'It will take several days to journey to Gretna Green and we will have to go in my curricle. I will be sure to find suitable hostelries on the way and you will have your own room so it will all be quite proper until we are married. After the ceremony, we will make our way back to Gloucester and take up residence in the small house which my father has found for me. I understand that it is very near Lord Shurlock's town house. What did you say?'

Delia had heard a whisper from Katy, but could not catch the words. Anthony's reply was clear enough.

'I will buy you everything you need, do not worry your pretty little head about that. Now this is the part you must remember especially well. It will be this coming Sunday morning, make an excuse not to go to church with your parents . . . no, it does not matter if it's broad daylight. I want to drive as far as possible on the first day . . . what did you say? No, you can bring a small portmanteau and it will be put behind. Please will you listen and not keep interrupting.

'While your family is at church, I want you to walk down that path that leads from your stables to the back of the gatehouse. No-one will see you and it is not far. Now think very hard, Katy. You know where that path comes out on to the road? You do? Good. On the other side of the road is a group of tall elms, a lot of bushes, too, just in the curve of the road.

'You are to cross the road and wait under the elms, you will be well hidden there even on a bright morning. Stay quite still and I will soon be there to pick you up. We will go down those lanes which lead to the Worcester turnpike, after that we will be on fast roads . . . what was that?

'Yes, I do have it all worked out, it only needs you to be courageous and a little daring. I do think that you will be daring for my sake. So let me say it again, as soon as the family have left for church, walk down the path, cross the road and wait under the elms. I will be there. You trust me? Let me kiss you before I go and . . . '

Delia did not wait for any more, she heard what she had come to hear. In hurrying off so quickly, she missed the rest of their conversation and the most important part.

By the time Katy came in the front door, it was almost dark. Delia thought she looked troubled, but that she also had an air of suppressed excitement about her.

'Katy, I was just coming to look for you, it is nearly dark.'

Katy's voice was tremulous. 'It was so nice and cool out there. I sat in the summer house and almost forgot the time.'

Be sensible, Delia was telling herself, try to make light of it. 'Do you remember when we used to take our books to the summer house when it was wet?' she asked lightly. 'Ambrose and I were talking about it just the other day.'

'Dear Ambrose,' Katy said, and Delia looked at her sharply. She had sounded almost wistful and here she was planning an elopement with the young gentleman of her dreams.

* * *

In the next few days, there no change in their usual comings and goings, in spite of there being no sign of Anthony after his exchange of words with Sir James.

Delia watched Katy carefully. She could see the girl was flushed and happy, but no more than she could have expected considering the plans she had made with Anthony.

But Saturday came, and Delia observed a marked change as she saw Katy's mood swing from laughing excitability to a nervous edginess all within a few minutes.

By the evening, Delia decided to put her plan into action and she was helped by Katy seeming to be unwell. She had eaten little at dinner and when she had refused one of her favourite fruit creams, it became obvious to her sister that Katy was beginning to feel nervous about the venture. When she went upstairs to bed before nine o'clock, Delia was not surprised and followed her half-an-hour later.

In the bedroom, Delia noticed immediately that there was no sign of a portmanteau and guessed that it was packed in readiness and tucked under the bed out of sight.

'Are you quite well, Katy?' Delia asked quietly. 'You have come up to bed early and I noticed that you refused your fruit cream at dinner. You are flushed, too. Do you think you are sickening for something?'

Katy was irritable, unusual for her. 'It is nothing, Delia, don't fuss. You are like a mother hen. I have the headache, that is all, but I am sure I shall never sleep.'

It was the opening which Delia had needed, she had not expected it to come so easily.

'I will go and get you a little laudanum, Katy. Would you like it in some weak brandy and water?'

Katy smiled. 'I think I would be glad of that, Delia, thank you very much. I will take it straight away and I am sure I will have a good night's sleep and feel better in the morning. It is just beginning to hit me that Papa will not allow Anthony to come. It cannot be possible that I shall not see him again. Something is sure to happen to make Papa think differently, I am confident of that.'

Delia, somewhat shocked at Katy's cool lying, went downstairs. She told her mother what she was going to do and poured some brandy into a glass.

'Thank you, dear,' Lady Stockdale said. 'The laudanum is in that cabinet in my bedroom, take care how you measure it, you will only need a few drops.'

Delia had looked in her mother's book which bore the title, *A Herbal For The Treatment Of Childhood Ailments* to try to find the correct dose of laudanum to use to suit her needs. She was firm in her intention of giving Katy enough laudanum to make her sleep until the middle of the following morning. It proved not to be an easy task as she knew that only a few drops of the drug was required for the toothache or for a good night's sleep.

Upstairs again, Delia found that Katy had undressed and was already in her nightgown and climbing into bed.

'Here is the brandy, Katy,' she said. 'I hope I have not made it too strong for you.'

'Thank you, Delia, I am sure I will sleep well.' She was sitting up and took the glass from her sister. She took a sip and made a face. 'It tastes odd, but I will sip it slowly. Do not wait, Delia, I promise to drink it all.'

Delia hesitated. She had wanted to be sure that Katy finished the whole glassful of the mixture, but felt that she could not very well stand over her until it was all gone. Katy was taking small sips without complaint, so Delia felt that it was safe to leave. She said goodnight and went downstairs again.

Delia was not to know it for a very long time, but as soon as her sister had shut the door, Katy spat out a mouthful of liquid into the glass. She had swallowed nothing. She distrusted even a small amount of laudanum for she had to wake very early.

She was remembering Anthony's instructions when he had changed his mind about their arrangements.

'Katy,' he had said. 'Forget all that about meeting during morning service, there are too many dangers. Be under the elm trees as I told you, but make sure that you are there as soon as it is light, say five o'clock in the morning. I will be there, trust me.' All this was said after Delia had left the summer house and she was not to learn of the change of plan.

So it was, that Katy decided that she would stay awake. She did not find it difficult for her mind was racing. She also had to compose a note for her mama. This was not easy and kept her occupied for over an hour.

Daylight came at last, and thrusting aside the doubts of the intervening hours, she dressed herself, and pulled her ready-packed portmanteau from under her bed. In her darkest pelisse, she crept quietly downstairs and let herself out of the house by the door from the kitchen which was never locked. Even Cook was not stirring and Katy slipped unseen from The Furlongs.

4

Two hours after Katy's departure from The Furlongs, Delia awoke and decided to peep into her sister's bedroom to make sure that Katy was still sleeping soundly. She opened both doors very quietly and once in Katy's room stood rigid with shock.

Bedclothes pushed back, no sign of Katy and the glass of brandy with its dose of laudanum was untouched on the bedside table.

In a daze, Delia picked it up. It is as full as it was when I gave it to her, she thought, she cannot have swallowed any of it. What is she up to? Anthony told her to be ready when we had gone to morning service. Surely she cannot have gone already? Did they change their plans after I had left the summer house? She asked herself all these questions, then decided that Katy must have gone downstairs to find something to eat.

But she paused. No, there is her nightgown, she must be dressed. She looked then at Katy's pelisses, finding only her very fashionable blue one, but her everyday, dark pelisse was missing, so was the navy-blue bonnet.

Grimly, Delia looked around and it took only seconds to find the note propped up on the dressing-table. With trembling fingers, she picked it up. It was addressed to her mama, but she thought that she should read it before going to find her parents. She imagined that the note could only contain bad news.

Dear Mama,

Please don't be cross with me, but I have run off to marry Anthony. We love each other and he is taking me to Gretna Green so that we can be married.

Don't come after me for I shall be very happy and I will write and tell

you as we are settled in Gloucester
where Anthony has a good position
and his own house.

My love to you and Papa,
Katy.

Shocked, Delia looked carefully around
the room. She felt herself unable to act
upon Katy's note or to come to any
decision. She checked Katy's dresses and
found her best blue sarsenet missing
and her favourite reticule could not be
found, and the silver brush and mirror
from the dressing-table were missing,
too. Last of all, her portmanteau was
not in its usual place.

She has gone, she really has gone,
Delia kept telling herself. My plans
have come to nothing and now I must
think, and I have to tell Mama. Papa,
too. How am I going to do it?

She found that in her shock, she
could not hurry and she went back into
her own room to dress herself, she was
thinking carefully all the time.

The first thing is to find Netta, she

71

decided, and it must be before she has time to take Katy her morning chocolate. Netta was her mother's personal maid, but she did little tasks for Delia and Katy as well as her other duties.

Netta can be trusted, Delia thought. I will tell her the truth and then ask her to take some breakfast to Katy's bedroom. We will pretend that Katy has not recovered from the headache and it will give me time to think things through before I see Mama.

Oh, Katy, you silly, girl. Could you not see that Anthony would not do? I would willing give up Ambrose for you rather than have this happen. I doubt Anthony means marriage at all.

Thinking of Ambrose gave Delia her first sensible decision. I will send a note to Ambrose and ask him to come as soon as he can. He will know what to do and he will probably be willing to go after them and take me with him.

Her mind made up, Delia acted quickly. She sat at her writing desk and wrote a hurried note to Ambrose deciding not to say why she needed him. She knew that he would come.

Dear Ambrose,

Something unfortunate has occurred and I badly need your help. Please could you come to The Furlongs as soon as possible. I will not go to morning service.

Delia.

She sanded it and sealed it, then went downstairs to find Netta. Fortunately the maid was on her own and Delia was able to tell her what had happened and to give her the instructions for breakfast.

The next thing was to slip round to the stables where the boys were already preparing the horses to be put to the carriage for the short journey to the church.

She called the eldest to her. 'Jem, you are to take this note to Lord Coberley at Ashleigh Court. You are to give it to no-one else. If Lord Coberley happens to be out of the house, then please find him. I trust you to do your best.'

'Yes, Miss Delia, I'll saddle Rustler, he's the fastest. I'll be back as quick as I can.'

Back in the house, Delia ate a solitary and early breakfast. I must eat well, she told herself, for if I go after Katy when Ambrose comes, there is no knowing when we might have time for another meal.

By the time she had finished her breakfast, she was expecting Ambrose, but there was no sign of him. At the stables, Jem had not returned. Frowning, she walked back to the house.

She tried to compose herself quietly in the drawing-room, having told her mama the lie that Katy was in bed and that neither of them would be going to morning service. The truth will come soon enough, Delia told herself.

When she heard the knock at the front door, she gave a start and then a sigh of relief. Ambrose had come.

She opened the door herself rather than wait for the maid and the words burst from her. 'Ambrose, thank heaven . . . '

But the words were halted in a gasp of shock. Standing in front of her was not the familiar figure of Ambrose, but a complete stranger and the most handsome gentleman she had ever seen.

'Miss Katy Stockdale?' he asked, there was an urgency in his voice.

'No, I am not Katy, I am Delia,' she replied and knew that she sounded rude. 'Who are you?'

'I am Anthony Mayfield's uncle.'

Delia did not ask the stranger into the house, she stared at him. 'Anthony's uncle? Rubbish, you cannot possibly be his uncle, you are not a lot older than he is. But if you are his uncle, then where is he?'

A glint came into keen grey eyes. 'Would you mind asking me in, Miss Stockdale, and I will try and explain.'

Delia felt embarrassed. 'I am sorry, I should not have kept you standing on the doorstep. We may be at a pass, but I do know better than that. Please come into the drawing-room and if indeed you have news of Anthony, please will you keep your voice low. My parents are in the breakfast-room and Mama thinks that Katy is unwell upstairs.'

'Katy is not here?'

'No.'

'Then I am too late.'

They faced each other in the drawing-room. 'Might I know your name, sir?' asked Delia.

'I am Kester Mayfield.'

Delia looked at him. Extremely tall, dark hair brushed back, handsome yet rugged features, and wearing coat and breeches of an excellent cloth and cut.

'You really are a Mayfield?'

'Yes, I will explain the relationship later. Just tell me if your sister, Katy, has gone off with Anthony, if you please.'

Delia nodded. 'Yes, I believe she has done so, but I have no idea at what time. I found she was missing at seven o'clock and she had left a note for Mama. I am expecting my fiancé, Lord

Coberley, at any moment and I am hoping to go after them. I thought you were him. What do you know of the matter?'

'May we sit down?' he asked and it was curtly said.

'Yes, I am sorry. My manners seem to have flown with the shock of it all. Please tell me who you are and how you come to know about Katy and Anthony.'

Kester Mayfield was a gentleman of some thirty years of age and was the youngest brother of Sir John Mayfield of Pelham Grange near Winchcombe. As Sir John was now elderly, Kester managed his estate for him and lived apart from the family in his own home, Fulbrook House, in the grounds of the big house. He had never married and liked to tell his friends that he was waiting for the right young lady to make herself known to him.

In spite of being an uncle to Anthony Mayfield, he liked to think that Anthony regarded him more as an older brother. Kester had disapproved of Anthony's life in London and had been instrumental in bringing him back to Pelham Grange and had also helped Sir John in securing the post for Anthony in Gloucester.

He was aware of Anthony's meeting with Katy Stockdale and it had pleased him to see the young man going off each day to visit her. Kester knew of the Stockdales and hoped that perhaps an alliance with a Stockdale daughter would help to steady the young man. Anthony had not failed to tell him how pretty Katy was.

On the evening previous to his unexpected arrival on the doorstep of The Furlongs, Kester had enjoyed a good dinner prepared for him by Mrs Bygraves, his cook-housekeeper, afterwards strolling in the grounds between his house and the grange to check on some fences. On his return, he was surprised to find a curricle at his front door, one of his boys at the horses' heads.

Mrs Bygraves came hurrying to meet him. 'Oh, Mr Kester, thank goodness you've come. Some visitors looking for Mr Anthony, I put them in the drawing-room.'

Mystified, Kester walked into the house, noticing that the horses were a prime pair and the curricle a very smart turn-out. Whoever the unknown visitors were, they were certainly not paupers.

In the drawing-room, he was confronted by a handsome young gentleman dressed without fault or any ostentation and a very pretty young lady with fair curls under a straw bonnet and having an anxious look in her eyes.

'You have the advantage,' Kester said.

'Are you Kester Mayfield? We are looking for Anthony and he is not to be found at Pelham Grange. Sir John Mayfield sent us here saying that he was probably with you. I am sorry we intrude upon you. May I introduce myself as Lord George Winterson, my father is Viscount Somerton, and this is my wife, Elinor.

Kester was immediately put on his guard. He knew Winterson to be one of Anthony's London associates though he had no idea that the young gentleman was married. A few months ago, they had both been very much young men about town and not of good habits.

'I have heard Anthony speak of you, Lord Winterson and I am pleased to welcome you and your wife to Fulbrook House. May I offer you some refreshment, some wine, perhaps?'

'No, thank you, sir, we are staying at *The George* in Winchcombe and have just dined. I particularly wanted to see Anthony today as we make our way to Elinor's family near Bristol first thing tomorrow morning.'

Kester frowned. 'I have no idea of his whereabouts at present, but I shall be seeing him first thing tomorrow morning. Is there any message I can give him?'

'It is a matter of honour, sir.'

Kester looked puzzled. Never a duel, he thought.

He posed the question. 'You do not mean a duel, I hope.'

There came a hurried reply. 'No, no, nothing like that. It is a question of a private wager we had between us.'

'A wager?' Whatever is this all about, Kester was thinking. Some mischief which Anthony got himself into while he was on the town?

Lord Winterson nodded. 'Yes, do you happen to know if Anthony is married?'

'Married? Goodness gracious no. He is in no position to support a wife though I do happen to know that he has been paying particular attention to Miss Katy Stockdale of The Furlongs in Prestbury. I certainly have hopes there when Anthony is settled into his new post as secretary to Lord Shurlock in Gloucester.'

'Anthony, a secretary? Why, his father must have been leaning on him,' came the reply which Kester thought impertinent.

'What is this wager you speak of?' he asked. 'Some nonsense from your time in London?'

This seemed to please the young Winterson. 'You are right, sir. Had a wager. One hundred pounds on the first to be married at Gretna Green. Thought I might have won. Elinor and I just back from there, man and wife, have the certificate to prove it. It looks as though we got there first, too, so he owes me one hundred pounds.

'I will be honest and confess to a little deception. I already knew that Elinor had agreed to marry me when we made the wager and that Anthony was quite unattached. Looks as though he's found someone though. Wouldn't surprise me to learn that he's whisked her off to Gretna Green thinking that he will be the first.'

He flashed a smile at the quiet Elinor then added as an afterthought, 'My father will be pleased though, always on at me to continue the family line. I like to settle a wager though, I will give you my forwarding address in Bristol, if you wouldn't mind telling Anthony. He is very welcome to visit us at Elinor's home. Saxby Park in Long Ashton, only a few miles from the centre of the city.'

He rose as he spoke, gave Kester a card, then turned to his wife. 'Come along, my dear, we must not be late or we'll be locked out of *The George*.

Kester escorted them to their curricle and watched them bowl down the drive to join the Winchcombe road.

He frowned as he watched the curricle disappear. Where was Anthony? Surely his London crony could not have been correct when he said that Anthony was probably already on his way to Gretna Green?

Cursing his young nephew, but feeling concerned, Kester Mayfield walked across to Pelham Grange. It did not take him long to discover that the young man's curricle was missing and that neither Will, the coachman, nor any of the stable boys knew of his whereabouts.

I shall have to go and ask John, he told himself and made his way round the house to find his elder brother.

Nearly twenty years separated the two brothers, but they were good friends and the older John relied on Kester for everything.

He found John and his wife, Margaret, taking tea before retiring for the night.

Sir John Mayfield had been handsome in his youth and was now a distinguished looking gentleman approaching sixty years with striking white hair, worn long and tied at the back with a black ribbon. He looked up and gave a frown when he saw that his visitor at that late hour was Kester.

'Kester, this is late for you, is something wrong?' he asked carefully.

'It is Anthony,' Kester replied. 'Do you happen to know where he is? His curricle is missing.'

'Anthony? Not in any trouble, I hope, he seems more settled at the moment and quite prepared to take up his duties in Gloucester. Margaret and I have thought it to be something to do with his acquaintance with the Stockdales. A very respectable family, I knew Sir James in our young days. I like to think that they have been a good influence on Anthony since his return from London. Do you know where he is, dear?' he addressed his wife.

Lady Margaret smiled. 'He went off very cheerfully after dinner,' she said. 'He said something about meeting young Hackett at some tavern called the *Boar's Head*. Why are you so concerned, Kester? We are used to Anthony coming home in the early hours, he does not seem to come to any harm, except that he drinks more wine than is good for him.'

Kester knew that he could make no mention of the wager and the visit of the young Wintersons. He would have to think of an excuse as quickly as he could.

'It is nothing. I had noticed that his hunter was lame and I wanted to warn him not to take him out tomorrow morning. One of the lads is preparing a poultice and I think the horse should be rested for a few days. I will come over early in the morning, though no doubt he will be sleeping off the effects of too much wine and brandy at the *Boar's Head*. I think it is over Gretton way, I hope he will take care down those narrow lanes after dark.'

Sir John gave a genial laugh. 'For all Anthony's faults, we will have to admit to him being a very good horseman, a top sawyer as they say in London circles. I think that you can take some credit for that, Kester.'

Kester nodded, but his mind was elsewhere. 'Sorry to have disturbed you both. I will bid you goodnight and I will come and look for Anthony in the morning.'

He walked slowly back to Fulbrook House. Something havey-cavey, he was telling himself. I don't doubt Winterson's story and I think the only thing I can do it so get some sleep and be up early in the morning to find out if Anthony is safely home.

He did sleep, but for longer than he

intended to and it was past eight o'clock before he was back at Pelham Grange.

He found the house in an uproar. His sister-in-law was sitting at the breakfast table, dabbing her eyes while trying to take sips of hot chocolate.

'Kester, I was about to send for you, but you said that you would come early. Such a to-do. I really don't know how to tell you . . . ah, John, there you are.'

Sir John appeared and it could be seen at a glance that he was in a rage. 'That wretched boy, what will he do next? Thought he had left his London ways behind him — no such good fortune. Blast, I've given him more money than I have to any of my children and I suppose that is where I went wrong. Read this, Kester, just found it in the library. He must have crept home last night and left it there . . . at least he had the decency to tell his mama what he was up to. Not that it helps . . . there dear,' he put his hand on his wife's shoulder. 'Try and drink your chocolate. All is not lost, Kester is here now.'

Kester had taken the small piece of paper and read the bold words with a sinking heart. He was too late.

Dear Mama,
   Just to let you know that I am going to marry Miss Katy Stockdale. We do not want a fuss so I am taking her to Gretna Green. I hope you will love her as I do.
   Anthony.

Kester made up his mind instantly, but still made no mention of the wager. 'I will go after them. I will go and see the Stockdales, I believe they live in Prestbury, I will soon be there. Leave it all to me, Margaret, I will do my very best.'

Lady Margaret wiped her eyes yet again. 'Thank you, Kester, thank you. I really don't know what we would do without you.'

Kester had to think quickly. He hurried back to Fulbrook house, gave the orders to put his pair of horses to the curricle, and went into the house to pack a small valise. It was possible he might have to find a lodging that night. But the most urgent need was to get straight to the Stockdales at The Furlongs in Prestbury.

The whole of this story was told to Delia as she and Kester Mayfield sat together in the drawing-room. Her mother had not appeared and Delia was thankful.

As Kester finished speaking, Delia felt as though her head was whirling with the impact of the tale. That Anthony could have run off with Katy to settle a wager was beyond belief.

She lifted her head to find grey eyes regarding her steadily and she felt reassured. Then she remembered that Ambrose had not yet appeared.

'It is a lot to take in, Mr Mayfield, I find I am very shocked and I still do not understand how you can possible be Anthony's uncle.'

He laughed and there was an easing of tension between them. 'It is quite simple Sir John Mayfield, Anthony's father, is the eldest of a very large family. I am the youngest of that family and there are nearly twenty years between us. He is a good brother to me and I manage his estate for him. I live on my own at Fulbrook House in the grounds of Pelham Grange. Now you will be able to work it out for yourself; there are only eight years between Anthony and myself. We are indeed, more like brothers.'

Delia found that she could smile for a moment. But only for a moment, for the thought of Anthony had brought back the thought of Katy.

'Do you know that they have already left?' Kester asked her.

She nodded and told him about Katy's note and how she had overheard them planning it all and had been determined to try and stop them.

'It all went wrong,' she said ruefully, 'and I was so careful with the laudanum not to give her too much. I saw her take a few sips and thought she would drink it, but I must have made her suspicious for by seven o'clock this morning, there was no sign of her . . . and Ambrose hasn't come either.'

'Who is Ambrose?'

'He is Lord Coberley and I am engaged to be married to him . . . '

'You are engaged? . . . A pity, I was just beginning to think that you might do for me.'

Delia stood up. 'How dare you, sir. To make such a frivolous remark when we are in such trouble.'

She walked to the window. She had thought she heard wheels on the gravel and was thankful to see Ambrose's curricle appear in front of the house.

'Oh, here is Ambrose now. He will know what to do.'

Delia ran to the front door and in seconds, an anxious Ambrose was in the drawing-room.

'What is it, Delia? And who, might I ask, is this gentleman?'

5

Delia introduced Ambrose to Kester Mayfield and the two gentlemen shook hands, albeit rather stiffly.

'Well, Delia, what is this matter of urgency? I imagine it must be something to do with Anthony if his uncle is here.'

'Ambrose, I am afraid you will be shocked,' Delia spoke as calmly as she could. 'Katy has eloped with Anthony, they are on their way to Gretna Green to be married.'

'Oh, my poor little Katy,' Ambrose said, and Delia looked at him sharply. He had sounded not only shocked, but as though it was a personal loss to himself. Then he straightened up and spoke sternly. 'Tell me everything you know, Delia.'

She told him from the beginning and included Kester's part in it. When it came to the question of the wager, she thought the solid Ambrose was going to lose his temper.

'A wager? What in the name of God almighty is he thinking of? My poor little darling. I must go after them as soon as possible.' He looked at Kester. 'Thank you for coming here, Mayfield, between us we might save the little girl from disgrace. Let me think.'

Kester broke in on Ambrose. 'It is my intention to go after them straight away, I have packed a valise. They have only a few hours start on us and it is easy to follow a route to Gretna Green. If you will excuse me, I will start off immediately. There is no time to be lost.'

But Ambrose was shaking his head and Delia was making a protest. 'But I must come, too, Katy will need me,' she pleaded.

Her fiancé was suddenly decisive. 'No, Delia, it will not do. If you will agree. Mayfield, I will set off now. I can pick up a few things at Ashleigh Court on the way. I have a very fast pair of horses and will be quicker on my own. I will ask you to follow with Delia, to call at every hostelry you pass to ask after them. I can be beyond Worcester by evening, I might catch them before they reach Kidderminster. Are you both agreeable to that?'

Delia looked at Kester Mayfield and he nodded. 'It is a sensible plan and I would enjoy having you with me, Miss Stockdale. You have yet to explain the situation to your parents and that will all take time. It will be better if Lord Coberley goes ahead.'

Delia had no difficulty in making up her mind. Something was going on in Ambrose's head and in his manner and she had the instinct that to send him flying after Katy was the right thing to do.

'Yes, please go ahead, Ambrose. I will come with you, Mr Mayfield, as soon as I have told Mama, that is. It is not going to be easy.'

Ambrose hurried out muttering, 'My

dear little Katy'. He even forgot himself and did not bid them goodbye.

When he had gone, Kester looked at Delia. 'Are you really going to marry that gentlemen? It would seem he is the more attached to Katy than to you! And may I call you Delia?'

She managed a grin. 'I thought I was going to marry him, but Katy certainly seems to be first in his thoughts at he moment. He is a good man, Katy will be safe with him if he can catch up with them.'

'I think you deserve something better than a 'good man', Delia. Let us try and introduce a little romance into the situation. You will come with me?'

She looked at him. 'I regard this situation as disastrous and certainly not romantic, sir, and might I remind that I have known you only for five minutes?'

'A very precious five minutes in my eyes, but I must not tease, you. We will have the seriousness that the situation demands. I promise to do my best for your sister and the first thing is to find your mother and father.'

'Yes, Mr Mayfield.'

'Kester, if you please.'

Delia did as requested. Unbidden, had come to her, a fascination for this gentleman who had entered her life less than an hour ago.'

'Yes, Kester.' She said to him with a pretended demureness. 'Now I will go and bring Mama and Papa into the drawing-room. Be prepared for hysterics.'

Sir James and Lady Patricia Stockdale were pleased to meet the brother of Sir John Mayfield, but when they heard the purpose of this visit, there was pandemonium at The Furlongs.

'My Katy, my Katy,' Lady Patricia wailed, while Delia hunted for the harts-horn.

Sir James lost his temper and shouted and railed against Anthony until he received some reassurance from Kester.

'The wicked girl, to think that a daughter of mine would run off to Gretna Green and all because I had refused an offer from a young whipper-snapper straight from the flesh-pots of London. He has disgraced the name of Mayfield and now my daughter has the audacity to run off with him.

'Yes, yes, Mayfield, I know that you will go after them and it is good to learn that Ambrose is already in pursuit . . . ' he turned to Delia. 'Leave your mama to me, run and get your pelisse and bonnet and whatever else you might need. I trust you with this gentleman, though why I should ever trust a Mayfield again, I cannot imagine. You will bring her home and she will have to be married properly in the church at Prestbury to the young devil, at least he's a Mayfield, I suppose that counts for something . . . '

Delia left him ranting and raving and ran upstairs for her portmanteau which she had packed in readiness, expecting to go off with Ambrose. The plan had changed, but she was still eager to be on her way.

Kester helped her into the curricle

and stowed away the portmanteau. They set off down the drive with a silence between them. It could be noted for its grimness until it seemed that Kester Mayfield was determined on good humour.

'Delia, we must try to be cheerful and hopeful. I am ashamed of Anthony's behaviour, but you must remember that it is nothing new to me. Twice I have journeyed up to London to get him out of jail for drunkenness and disorderly behaviour. I was pleased when I at last persuaded him to come home to Winchcombe.'

'But you do not know about the wager,' she reminded him.

He gave a frown. 'No, I suppose I must blame myself for being taken in. I was particularly fooled when he put off his foppish ways and started to dress himself with some respectability to go and visit your sister. It just suited his plans when he met Katy at her come-out.'

'Were you there?' she asked curiously.

'Yes, but I was in the card room. I do not dance. If I had known that you were there, I might have attempted the country dance at least.' He glanced down at her, he admired her looks and the sense she had shown that morning.

'Balderdash,' she replied with some amusement. 'You had better look to your horses, this lane is very narrow.'

'Certainly, Miss Stockdale,' said one of the country's best drivers. 'I will remind you that we will soon be on the turnpike road to Worcester and we have promised the admirable Ambrose to call at any inns on the way. He will be way ahead of us by now, I wonder if he has caught up with his Katy.'

* * *

Ambrose had not caught up with Katy, for Katy was having an unhappy time of it with an Anthony who was driving along the turnpike road as though his life depended on it. He took corners dangerously and overtook other vehicles with scarcely an inch to spare.

Everything had gone according to plan, but after the first rush of excitement and success, Katy could feel only a miserable guilt.

She had reached the group of elms in minutes. It was only just light, but she could pick out the horses and the curricle under the trees. She ran the last few steps anxiously, then felt an immediate joy on hearing Anthony's voice.

'You have come, my love, how brave you are. Let me help you up.' His voice was reassuring and helped to calm her nervousness.

Once up beside him, she felt braver, even adventurous.

'Give me a kiss, my sweet,' Anthony said. His driving coat had four capes and she thought he looked very dashing.

'We should not, Anthony, not yet.'

He laughed and the besotted girl did not hear the falseness of it. 'I am not going to wait until we reach Gretna

Green for a kiss from you,' he declared and before taking up the reins, he pulled her close into his arms and his lips were on hers.

Katy had never been kissed with passion before and she felt alarmed, but the kiss over, Anthony held her closely to him for a moment.

'I cannot wait until you are my wife,' he whispered. 'The faster we go, the sooner that will be, so be prepared for us to speed along, my little Katy.'

Anthony concentrated on his whip and his horses and Katy was left with mixed feeling of excitement, happiness and anxiety. She kept thinking of her mama and began to wonder if Ambrose and Delia would come after them. One minute she found herself wishing that they would, then Anthony would take her hand and raise it to his lips and she knew the thrill of love and adventure.

They stopped at a respectable inn called *The Duke of Buckingham*, where they had a quick luncheon. Anthony was all kindness and attention, and

Katy began to trust him and to enjoy herself.

The next stop was in Worcester for an early dinner and Katy found that Anthony was inclined to rush her over the meal. He told her that he hoped to reach Kidderminster for the night.

The word, 'night' was enough to alarm Katy, and she asked Anthony where they would be staying. 'Have you got friends near Kidderminster, Anthony?'

He took her hand across the dining table. 'You are not to worry about anything, my love. I have it all arranged. We will be very comfortable and I will take care of you quite nicely. You do love me, Katy?'

His gaze was sincere, his grasp was reassuring. It made Katy wonder why her misgivings over the venture seemed to grow at every passing mile. But of one thing she was certain.

'Yes, I love you, Anthony, and you are taking care of me very nicely.'

'Good girl, we will be on our way

then. I am determined on reaching Kidderminster, for if your father comes in pursuit of you, he would never dream we could have reached Kidderminster in a day. We have made surprisingly good progress and you have been a very good passenger.'

'Ambrose might come after me,' Katy said.

'Ambrose?' Anthony's voice rose at the name. He had met Lord Coberley and had not liked him, considering him to be a bore. 'Why should Ambrose pursue you?'

'I think he loves me.'

Anthony, although anxious to be on the move, could not let Katy's statement pass without some comment.

'What are you saying, Katy? Ambrose is engaged to marry Delia, their wedding arranged.'

'Yes, I know, but it is the way he looks at me sometimes. I am sure that if I had been older, he would have chosen me,' she told him quite calmly.

'You are talking nonsense, Katy, and

you have chosen me. Let us be off.'

Katy felt unsettled on the next stage of their journey. She thought of Ambrose a lot of the time. He would be shocked at her running off with Anthony. Ambrose would never have done such a thing, she told herself. I wonder if he will come after me?

Then her thoughts turned to how angry her papa would be and her mama would be upset. She was sure Delia had tried to stop her running off by giving her the laudanum, though she could not imagine how Delia had guessed about the elopement. She would not be surprised to find Ambrose and Delia chasing after her.

But a glance up at the handsome, determined face of Anthony and her feeling of pleasure when he turned his head to give her a smile, made her feel uncertain that she had chosen the right way and the right person.

By the time they reached the town of Kidderminster, the sun was low in the sky and Katy was feeling tired. She was thankful when Anthony drove through the archway of *The King's Arms*. The ostlers took the horses and Anthony led her to the front of the inn.

The landlord, a tall, thin, and rather serious looking man hurried forward and spoke pleasantly to them.

'Good evening, sir . . . and madam. How can I be of help?'

Anthony smiled confidently. 'Mr and Mrs Anthony Mayfield of Cheltenham. Have you a room for us for the night? We have already dined.'

Katy was tired and longing for her bed, but Anthony's words woke her with a start of alarm and horror.

'No, no, Anthony, I must have my own room. We are not . . . '

She felt Anthony's hand on her arm in a hard grip. 'My love, don't be shy with me, of course we must share a room now that we are man and wife.' With these words, he drew her to one side and hissed at her. 'Don't be missish now. You agreed to run away with me and I have not the money for two rooms. A few days makes no difference and it will be very cosy to be together, Katy.'

Katy screamed. 'You are wicked. I thought you were loving and all the time, you were wicked. I won't stay . . . '

Her words were lost for she had wrenched her arm from Anthony's grasp and rushed to the door.

Katy was small and could move quickly. She was running away from the *King's Arms* in a flash. She turned down the street not even noticing that she was running in a different direction from the one they had entered the town. She ran as quickly as her long pelisse and skirts would allow. She heard Anthony's voice, then silence and she guessed that he had gone for the curricle.

I must hide somewhere, she was saying frantically as tears threatened to blind her. She glanced round quickly and found herself in a street of small shops, her heart sank, they would offer her no cover. She ran again expecting the curricle to overtake her at any minute.

The buildings stopped and she realised that she was under trees. She slowed down and saw that they were the yews of a churchyard. Through the gate, she could see the large, stone slabs of the grave stones. She did not stop to think, she was in the churchyard and cowering behind the largest stone she could find, clinging to it in her fright.

Katy was not to know it, but Anthony was searching for her on the road back to Worcester, assuming that it was the way she would have run, but in her panic, she had run in the opposite direction and was sheltering in the churchyard of the Kidderminster parish church.

★　★　★

Katy later learned that Anthony, not being able to find her, drove through the night without resting his horses. He entered Pelham Grange in the early hours without being seen. He gathered together the most suitable garments he possessed, put them in the curricle and was off again within minutes. Without any regrets or further thought for Katy and his wager, he was on his way to his new post and new house in Gloucester.

On that night of Katy's elopement, with no sign of Anthony, she had to decide what to do next. She dared not go back to the inn. She was disgraced and she had very little money.

Many thought of Katy as a silly girl for she often behaved so, but she did possess a streak of commonsense and her wilfulness was easily turned to determination.

I will find shelter somewhere for the night, then as soon as it is light, I will start walking back towards Worcester and hope that a farm wagon will pass me and take me up. I have lost my portmanteau, but I still have my reticule with a few coins in it.

She looked around her and the

eeriness of the graveyard in the fading light did not alarm her. She was more aware that the old church was a solid stone building. I could shelter in the porch, she thought, or is it possible that the church might be kept open. She thought that she had read somewhere that a church, being a holy place, was regarded as a place of refuge and always kept open.

She got up and walked slowly and quietly towards the church. Inside the porch, the heavy wooden door opened easily and she closed it carefully behind her. She found herself almost in darkness, there was only a glimmer of light from the stained windows, but she could make out the pews and she knew she would be able to lie down, she might even find a hassock for her head.

She walked towards the nearest pew.

'Who is it then?'

A growl of a voice and afterwards, Katy thought that of all the things which had happened on that eventful day, this was the worst moment.

She did not turn and run and she never knew why. She seemed to be pinioned to the spot. She was getting used to the poor light and saw a tall figure coming towards her. She wondered if it was the rector, but then she became aware of the ragged clothes and the unkempt, unwashed smell of a tramp. She could not speak, something seemed to be blocking her throat. Neither could she move.

'I can see 'e, who is it then? Bless me, if it ain't a female. What you doing here then? You needn't be afraid o' me. I'm only old Jacob, I allus sleep here if I'm going by Kidderminster. Rector leaves church open and bread and water for the likes of us. He's a holy soul, that he is. Now you'd better tell me what it is. You in trouble of some sort?'

As she got nearer, she saw an elderly man, tall but rather bent, she guessed his skin to be very brown. He had spoken kindly and he was regarding her kindly and in her particular distress, she trusted him. But I'm not going to tell the truth, she decided.

And imitating the voice of her mother's maid, she told her tale.

'It's like this, mister, I'm maid to Miss Sophie at the big house.' She thought it safer to say that. 'A right lovely young lady she is, too, but her brother, he's a devil. Won't leave me alone, catches me anywhere, kisses me sometimes more familiar. I thought it were one them things a maid had to put up with from the son of the house, so I said nothing. But, mister, tonight it were different, came into my little room, he did.

'I got away and ran downstairs and found one of my Miss's pelisses and ran off and this were the only place I could think of to shelter. I thought as rector left door open. Suppose I'd better be off, seeing as you're here.'

'What are you going to do next then?' he asked, making no comment about her story.

'I'll get a few hours sleep, then I'll start and walk to Worcester. I got an aunt there.'

'And what's your name, miss?'

'Janey.'

'Well, Janey, you needn't be afeard of me as I told you. You lie down on one of them pews and I'll get you a hassock for your head. And I'll settle at the front of the church and in the morning, then we'll share the bread atween us. Fellow travellers, you might say, then I'll walk along the turnpike with you and I'll stop the first wagon as is going to Worcester market.'

'You are very kind,' Katy said, thinking that in this wicked escapade, some good was shining on her.

'Well, it's a bit unusual sharing the church with a serving maid. I've shared with the likes of myself and I've shared with mice and bats, but never a young lady. You'll come to no harm o' me so don't you go running off again when it's nearly dark outside.'

'No, I won't, thank you very much,' she said, forgetting to use her maid's voice, but he did not seem to notice.

He fetched her a hassock and left her

to settle herself, he did as he said he would and walked to the front of the church and she heard him stretch himself out and mutter something as though he was saying his prayers.

I'm too wicked to say my prayers, Katy thought sadly, but I hope God will forgive my foolishness and I do pray for Mama and Papa and Delia . . . and Ambrose, she added.

The pew bench was very uncomfortable, but Katy was so weary that she slept immediately and soundly. She was awakened by the sun streaming through the window over the altar. Her first thought was that the coloured rays from the sun were beautiful.

That was before she remembered the predicament she was in. Anthony. How could he have done it? Telling the innkeeper that they were man and wife and asking for a room for them to share. And I did love him, she told herself, I was sure I loved him, but all the tales that had gone before him were true.

He is nothing but a rake and a rascal, saying that he would take me to Gretna Green and then pretending that I was his wife before we even got there.

She sat up. She could hear the dawn birds from the churchyard and the sound was lovely to her. Inside the church, all was silent and she wondered if the old man had gone. I think I will creep away, I can start walking to Worcester on my own. I must try and forget about food, at least I did have dinner last night.

She heard the click of the door and felt herself go rigid.

Then a voice said, 'So you'm awake, young lady. I crept out for a wash at the village pump and tried not to disturb 'e.'

She looked at him walking towards her. He was not as old as she had thought him to be in the half-light of the previous evening, and now his long hair was washed and his face clean and shining.

'I've saved some bread for 'e, I don't

114

suppose you ever breakfasted on a slice of bread afore, and there's a drink of water. I fetched a clean cup from the vestry.'

'Thank you,' she replied. 'Do you know what time it is?'

'Seven o' clock by the church clock outside,' he said. 'We'll be on our way if you'm still going to do as you said you was.'

She looked at him curiously. He was a puzzle, he did not seem like the ordinary vagrant. His speech was rough, but his manners were kindly.

'How did you come to be a tramp like this,' she asked him, then tried to recover herself and her speech. 'You ain't like them we had at the kitchen door of the big house always begging.'

'Finish your bread and I'll tell you as we walk along. I'll walk slow like, so as you can keep up with me.'

They were soon on the Worcester road and walking in pleasant country-side. It was too early to be busy on the road and no farm cart passed them.

I must be patient, thought Katy, I am sure I will be home in Prestbury before the day is out, and she tried not to think of the wrath she must expect from her father. All thoughts of Anthony, she tried to put behind her. She enjoyed listening to her companion.

'I were a gardener in a big house,' he told her, 'but I were struck down with the rheumatics so I had to leave, the trouble was I had to leave my little cottage as well. I never did marry and when that happened, I were glad I only had myself to look after. So for weeks now, I've been walking a few miles each day, picking up a bit of work here and there. Now I'm on my way to the Vale of Evesham for the fruit season, by the time I get there, first strawberries'll be ready . . . ' he stopped suddenly. 'Miss, there's a curricle across the road and looks like a gentleman's shouting to us.'

Katy looked and could not believe her eyes. Nor her ears.

'Katy, Katy,' came the sound of her name being called out. She looked again.

It was Ambrose.

6

Lord Coberley had experienced a very trying time during the previous twenty-four hours. He had left Prestbury thinking that he would catch up with Katy and Anthony in no time at all, but although his horses gave of their best, he reached Worcester without catching sight of the runaway pair.

There, he decided to stop for a luncheon and then to spend time looking round the city, for it was the most likely place for Katy to want to stop. He knew that they would be forced to spend a night somewhere in the vicinity and he hoped to catch up with them before Katy committed this impropriety.

He made sure that he had a substantial luncheon for there was no knowing when he would get his dinner, and he proceeded to drive out of

Worcester in the direction of Kidder-minster.

It was on this road that things started to go wrong. He spotted a curricle in front of him travelling at great speed. There were two people up front and one of them seemed to be a young lady. He also had the feeling that the horses were very much like Anthony's pair of matched bays which had been seen at The Furlongs many times during those past few weeks.

He pressed his own pair of horses and overtook the suspicious curricle only to find that it was driven by an older man and with a girl young enough to be his daughter.

In a few moments, Ambrose was cursing this excessive speed, for one of his own horses slowed up and showed signs of lameness. He stopped at the nearest coaching house knowing that he would have to rest his horses until the morning.

Resigned to this set-back, he ordered an early dinner, drank a bottle of wine with it and retired to his room before nine o'clock, intending to be on the road again before breakfast in the morning.

He tried to put all thoughts of Katy and Anthony to the back of his mind, but it was not easy, for he knew that he had failed in trying to stop them from having to lodge somewhere for the night. Katy had no maid with her, and he did not trust Anthony Mayfield.

★　★　★

Next morning, he awoke refreshed, ordered some coffee to be brought to his room, but refused breakfast.

His horses seemed to be recovered and he set off hopefully. His was the only curricle on the road and he made good progress. It was as he approached the town of Kidderminster that he saw the two figures walking towards him. They were on the other side of the road and he could see immediately that the man

119

of the pair was a rough vagrant. But surely . . .

Ambrose pulled up his horses abruptly and looked again. The young lady walking at the vagrant's side looked like Katy, there was no doubt about it. But how could it be Katy? She was with Anthony.

But a sudden laugh and a toss of the head told him that indeed it was his Katy. But what in the devil's name was she doing walking along the turnpike at this hour of the morning with a man who was no more than a tramp?

He called her name clearly and saw her stop. He could see the look of amazement in her face and he heard her call his name.

'Ambrose . . . oh, it is you . . . oh, Ambrose.'

She came running across to his curricle and he jumped down quickly and took her in his arms.

Katy felt Ambrose's strong arms around her and knew that she was safe. She felt tears come to her eyes and she buried her head against his driving coat. She could hear his words clearly.

'Katy, my little love, I have found you. But whatever are you doing walking along the turnpike at this hour? Where is Anthony? And whoever is this that you are with?'

Katy looked up at last, her eyes were moist and shining.

'Ambrose, I have never been so glad to see anyone in my life. And you must meet Jacob, he has been so good to me . . . Jacob, please come,' she shouted to the astonished man who was gazing at them from the other side of the road.

Ambrose looked shocked when he saw the roughness of the man, but there was something about the weather-beaten face which was honest. He listened to Katy's excited chatter and kept a firm hold on her.

'Ambrose, I cannot tell you the whole story now, but Anthony is very wicked, I was quite deceived. I ran away from him and hid in the church, it was the only place I could find, and I was frightened because it was nearly dark and there was someone in there, but it was only Jacob. He often sleeps there and the rector leaves him bread and water and Jacob gave me some of the bread.

'Oh, I forgot to say that all this happened last night and I slept in the church, but Jacob was in the front pew and I was in the back. And he is on his way to the Vale of Evesham for the fruit picking and he was going to stop a farm wagon for me when one came along and I was going to try and get back to Prestbury. But now you have come and, Ambrose, I am very hungry with having no breakfast . . . '

She stopped suddenly and turned to Jacob. 'I am sorry, Jacob, I did not tell you the truth. I am not a lady's maid and I ran off from my home with a young gentleman and he deceived me and I ran away from him and you know what happened next. This is Lord Coberley and I have known him all my life and he is going to marry my sister.'

Katy paused at last and Ambrose looked at Jacob. It seemed that Katy had been fortunate in her protector however rough he looked.

'We are in your debt, sir,' he said. 'Can we take you as far as Worcester?'

Jacob grinned. 'Never ridden in a curricle in my life,' he replied with a grin, 'and I don't suppose I ever will. But I thank'e and I'm glad the little lass has found you and I'll be on my way. And you can tell Miss Janey that I suspicioned that she were a lady and not a lady's maid.'

Ambrose looked at Katy and she gave a grin. 'I pretended I was a maid,' she whispered. He shook his head in despair, then wrestled with the question of whether he would offend Jacob if he offered money.

'I cannot thank you enough, Jacob. I know you would have protected Katy without accepting a penny, but here are a couple of guineas to buy yourself some food before you reach Evesham. You will find plenty of work there at this time of year.'

Jacob made no fuss and slipped the coins into a capacious pocket.

'Thank 'e kindly, sir, it don't go amiss. And Miss Janey, I wish you well with your friend, it's a relief to me to see you safe. I'll be on me way now.'

He walked off without another glance and Katy watched him go before Ambrose helped her up into the curricle.

'Ambrose, just think about it. There is Anthony dressed like the perfect gentleman and behaving like a rake and a reprobate, and tattered old Jacob behaving as the gentleman he is at heart.' She looked at him as he took up the reins. 'Did you come looking for me, Ambrose? I could not believe it when I heard your voice. What are we going to do now? I have a lot to tell you.'

Ambrose smiled and she knew that she could see love and affection in his eyes. 'I imagine that you quarrelled with Anthony in Kidderminster, so I think we will repair to the hostelry there, I believe it to be called *The King's Head*, and you can tell me your story over breakfast. I might tell you that I also have gone without breakfast to come looking for you, so I will welcome a good meal. Why do you look worried?'

Katy did not know how to tell him the truth, but she had done so many wrong things that truth seemed to be the only way forward.

'I don't think I can go back to *The King's Head*, Ambrose. You see, Anthony took me there and he told the landlord that I was his wife and he asked for one room for us. I hadn't thought him to be wicked until that moment, but I ran away from him and that's how I came to hide in the church. Oh, and my portmanteau is still at the inn.'

Ambrose tried not to show the anger he felt at Anthony's behaviour.

'We will have to tell the landlord a little untruth, Katy. I will say that you are my sister-in-law, for you will be one day if I marry Delia, and that you ran away from home. I have come to take you back, I will tell him, and then I will order a good breakfast for us both.

'You have behaved very badly, Katy. It is such a relief to have you safe that I am inclined to forget your shocking behaviour. After breakfast, we will travel as quickly as we can back to Prestbury and put your poor mama's mind at rest.'

'Yes, Ambrose,' Katy whispered, and it was in a very small voice indeed. She reached up and kissed his cheek. 'Thank you for coming after me.'

★ ★ ★

Ambrose drove as quickly as he could into Kidderminster and soon found *The King's Head*. He left the curricle in the yard and took Katy round to the front of the inn. He thought she looked nervous and ashamed and had no sympathy for her.

The landlord was found. He took in

the splendour of Ambrose's riding coat and looked with astonishment at the young lady at his side.

Ambrose was impressive. 'Lord Coberley, Ashleigh Court in Gloucestershire,' he announced himself. 'This is Miss Katy Stockdale, daughter of Sir James and Lady Stockdale of Prestbury, she is my sister-in-law. As you can see, she is very young and has behaved most foolishly, but you will know that she ran away from the young gentleman she was with and you will have guessed that he was not her husband.

'She managed to find shelter for the night and fortunately I have found her. You might serve us a good breakfast and I believe you have Miss Stockdale's portmanteau here. I am taking her back to her parents immediately we have finished our breakfast. The dining-room?'

'This way, my lord,' the landlord said, who was, in fact, rather relieved to see the young lady safe. 'And I have the portmanteau here.'

Katy was expecting Ambrose to be angry with her, especially so as they were on their own in the small dining-room.

'I am so sorry, Ambrose,' she said quietly, seeking to allay his wrath. 'I know I have been silly and I hope Mama will forgive me.'

'But, Katy, whatever possessed you to do such a thing?'

'Anthony was so young and handsome and it upset me when Papa refused him when he asked to marry me. I know he had been a little wild in London, but most young gentlemen like to spend some time on the town, as they say, and he did have a good post to go to in Gloucester.

'When he suggested that we ran off to Gretna Green, I thought it was so exciting. Once we were married we would be quite respectable. But it went wrong, you see, and when Anthony told the landlord that I was his wife and said we were to share a room, I was shocked. I was really shocked,

Ambrose, and I think I was frightened. All I could think of was that I must run away from him.

'Then you came, Ambrose. When I saw you in the curricle, I think it was the nicest thing that has ever happened to me and here we are having breakfast together . . . what is it, Ambrose? You suddenly look very serious.'

He nodded. He knew that he must tell her the truth, but it was not going to be easy, except that Mr Anthony Mayfield had already fallen off his pedestal as far as Katy was concerned.

He proceeded to tell her of Kester Mayfield's visit and the news that the gentleman had brought with him.

'I am afraid, Katy, that Anthony was not taking you to Gretna Green because he loved you, but because of a wager he had made with a crony of his in London.'

'A wager? Whatever do you mean?'

'The two young gentlemen made a wager that the first to marry a young lady at Gretna Green would win one-hundred pounds. Anthony has already lost the wager, because his friend arrived at Pelham Grange with his new wife straight from Gretna.'

Katy was round-eyed and slightly scared.

'However could he be so wicked? It was a wicked wager, Ambrose, to involve two young ladies like that and to think I might have married him. I can believe it though. After hearing him say that we were Mr and Mrs Mayfield to the landlord, I can believe anything.

'Oh, I am so sorry to have caused you all this trouble. You have come after me, and poor Mama will be in a fuss and Papa will be angry with me. And what about Delia? You did not bring her with you?'

'No, she is following with Kester Mayfield.'

'But he is Anthony's uncle even though I believe he is not a lot older. I did not ever meet him, but I know that Anthony had a regard for him. I believe it was Kester who helped Anthony's father to find the post with Lord Shurlock. I wonder if he will take it up now. But, Ambrose, why is Delia coming with Kester? I don't understand it. She is engaged to you.'

'She is engaged to me at the moment,' he said bluntly.

'Whatever do you mean?'

'I think I might be undergoing a change of heart, my dear,' he told her gently.

'You are saying that you don't want to marry Delia? You have fallen in love with someone else, Ambrose. You never did love Delia, she is more like a sister to you, I always thought so. Do I know the young lady? I could wish it might be me, but you would never marry me after me disgracing the family by running off with Anthony. Oh, how could I have been so foolish?'

Katy was frowning, but Ambrose smiled at her.

'It is easy to be persuaded when one loves someone as you thought you loved Anthony. I believe you thought only of the romance of it all and the excitement,' he said.

'Yes, it is true and now I see it all in a different light. Perhaps I have grown up a little. I don't know why you came after me, Ambrose, and you have not told me yet why you came on ahead of Delia and Kester Mayfield.'

'I wanted to be on my own so that I would be quicker,' he told her. 'Kester and Delia are stopping to ask after you at the coaching houses and inns on the way.'

'Oh, what a lot of trouble I have caused, all through my own foolish dreams. I wish I had never met Anthony Mayfield.'

'No, don't say that, Katy, it has brought me to you after all. Now we must finish with all this regret and be on our way.'

She smiled at him as she rose from the table and was struck by the happiness of his expression. It will be a lucky person who marries him, she told herself rather sadly, even if it means that Delia will lose him. She went up to him.

'Thank you for coming after me, Ambrose,' she whispered and reached up and kissed his cheek. She heard a sharp intake of his breath and the next instant, found herself in his arms.

'I think we can do better than that, little love,' he said and his lips were on hers in a kiss which started softly and gently enough, but which quickly turned to an embrace of love and passion.

'My Katy,' he said as the kiss came to an end.

Katy stared and she knew love in that instant. The kisses of Anthony Mayfield had been sweet, but had never aroused this deep feeling in herself. She had always thought her love for Ambrose to be a brotherly affair. Now she knew differently, but she could not admit it. There was Delia to consider.

'Ambrose,' she said, still close to him. 'I am the person you have fallen in love with, you said that you had had a change of heart. You do not love Delia?'

He gave a frown. 'I would never have told you, my sweet, but you were too tempting and you needed my protection. I have loved you for a long time, but you were very young and I settled for Delia. Then suddenly, Anthony Mayfield comes along and you grow into a beautiful and desirable young lady all in a few weeks.

'I should never had said anything to you for there is Delia to consider. I cannot ask you to marry me unless she cries off, and we have to think that the wedding is already planned. And there is another thing to consider, Katy.'

'What is that?' Katy's senses were swimming. She felt as though she had been in love, out of love and very near to loving again all within the space of a few days.

She thought she knew what Ambrose was going to say.

'I can't expect you to love me. I am older and you are only just recovering from your affair with Anthony.'

'I have forgotten Anthony,' she declared stoutly.

He laughed aloud and kissed her again. 'We must be sensible. No more talk of love. We have to get you back to your mama and the sooner we leave Kidderminster, the sooner we will be at The Furlongs. We will go and pick up your portmanteau and I must leave a message with the landlord for Kester and Delia in case they get this far.'

Ambrose settled his bill, thanked the landlord, then asked for a pen and a piece of paper and a standish.

'I am expecting a Mr Mayfield, he is a relative of the young gentleman who has caused us all this trouble, would you be good enough to give him this note. It is brief, but he will understand.

Mr Kester Mayfield,

I have Katy safe and we are on our way back to Prestbury.

Coberley.

★　★　★

The portmanteau was taken out to the curricle and the two of them set off. Throughout the journey, with Ambrose weaving in and out of slow farm wagons and heavy, cumbrous coaches, Katy was aware of how much more comfortable it was to be sitting next to Ambrose than it had been to accompany the man she thought she had loved.

I will not use the word wicked again, she told herself, I was just very foolish. Anthony had a bad reputation and Papa knew it. I took no heed and believed a young gentleman who was using me for his own ends. I suppose I was fortunate in that he betrayed his lecherous nature at the inn and I was able to run away from him.

It could have been that he fooled me all the way to Gretna Green and by that time, I would have been obliged to marry him to save my reputation. I have been foolish, but I will not call myself wicked.

Ambrose said very little. The road was busy and needed all his concentration, but they made good progress and reached Prestbury before dinner.

As they went through the lanes which would bring them out near The Furlongs, Katy began to feel nervous. Ambrose sensed it and put out a hand to her. She was glad to cling to him and he did his best to reassure her.

'Your mama will be overjoyed,' he told her. 'I will speak to your father and explain all the circumstances. I know he will say that it was as he had thought, but he will be glad to have you safely at home again.'

'Thank you, Ambrose, it has all happened in two days, it does not seem possible. I feel that you have become a different person to me.'

He squeezed her hand before taking up the reins again. 'And so I have, my little one.'

'Why do you call me that?' she asked him.

'Because that is what you are.' And he said no more until they reached The Furlongs.

Katy's mother had seen the curricle

from the drawing-room window and rushed to the front porch.

Katy jumped down without any help from Ambrose and ran into her mother's arms; they were both of them crying.

'Katy, Katy, why did you do it? And all because your papa refused Anthony. Come and tell me what has happened. And here is dear Ambrose, you found her and have brought her home, I will never be able to thank you. But what about last night, Katy? I dread to think what might have happened.'

Ambrose and Katy had decided to tell her mama the lie. The truth would have caused an attack of the vapours.

'Ambrose kindly got me a room at the *The King's Head* at Kidderminster, Mama, we had breakfast there and have hurried home.'

'But what about Anthony?'

This was more difficult. 'When Ambrose appeared, Anthony knew that he couldn't go on with me and I realised how foolish I had been. I think he is probably back at Pelham Grange by now. But what about Delia? Ambrose told me about Kester Mayfield, I did know of him. Have they not returned? We saw no sign of them.'

'No, we have not seen them so I hope they don't go all the way to Gretna Green.'

Katy shook her head. 'No, do not worry. They are sure to call at the *The King's Head* in Kidderminster. It is the main hostelry and Ambrose left a message for them to say he had brought me home.'

'Dear Ambrose,' Lady Stockdale said.

And Katy was inclined to echo the sentiment.

7

Delia, sitting up beside a gentleman she had not known an hour ago, was determined to make the best of an awkward situation.

'We will not have to stop at every inn which we pass, will we, sir?' she asked him and saw him frown.

'I would prefer you not to be formal with me, Delia. I think that we will fare better if we remember that our families have long been acquainted. We have not met before only because I am not the kind of person who enjoys visiting and balls and routs. I have work to do at Pelham Grange and it happens to be work which I love. I am a gentleman of the countryside and not of the ballroom.'

Delia listened to his serious voice with interest and amusement. If he was willing to talk then perhaps their pursuit of Katy and Anthony would not be quite so awkward and painful.

He did not wait for a reply, but answered her question. 'We can discount every little tavern and alehouse, it is only the larger inns which can provide for horses and carriages. We will call at those places and hope for news. You will be happy to hold the horses while I go and make the enquiries?'

'Yes, of course, I drive myself, but only the family trap. A phaeton does not seem to be a vehicle suited to muddy country lanes. In Cheltenham, it is different. I ride every day with Ambrose, but that is not quite the same as driving a vehicle.'

'You are engaged to Lord Coberley, you said, I believe?'

She looked up at him remembering his odd reaction when she had told him so. 'Yes, we are to be married in July and it is to be a quiet affair.'

'I thought him very disturbed at Katy's disappearance, are you sure he is to marry the right sister?'

Delia felt herself getting cross at his words.

'I would be glad if you would concentrate on the matter in hand sir, and not to speculate on the feelings and actions of Lord Coberley.'

'Certainly, ma'am,' he said evenly, his hands steady on the reins as they wove in and out of the heavy traffic. 'I believe we are about to join the turnpike road from Gloucester to Worcester and there are sure to be one or two coaching houses before we reach the city.' He paused as he swept past a lumbering barouche. 'With your permission I will concentrate on my cattle.'

Delia fell silent. He may be a Mayfield, she was telling herself, he may be quite handsome, but I do not think I am going to like this gentleman. But I must not think about Kester Mayfield. It is Katy who needs my first attention.

They stopped at *The Sorrel Horse*, they stopped at *The Green Dragon*, they stopped at *The Cavendish* and *The Malt Shovel*. Delia held on to the horses, then watched as Kester came out of each one shaking his head.

'They must have got as far as Worcester,' she told him after his last fruitless visit. 'I am getting hungry, are you?'

'Yes, I am, we will have a luncheon in Worcester whatever happens.'

But before they reached Worcester, the likely looking *Duke Of Buckingham* came into view.

'This looks more like it,' Kester said, as he drove into the stable yard. 'We will have some lunch here whether we have news of the wretched pair or not. I am getting tired of your silly sister and my rogue of a nephew. I'd rather sit in the dining-room and look at you, Delia.'

'There is no need for flattery, Kester, we are getting along tolerably well.'

But Delia wished that she had not said these words for Kester went into the hostelry and came out smiling.

143

'They were here an hour ago. A perfect description from the landlord who said that they took their meal in a hurry and went off in the direction of Worcester. That must be our next objective, Delia.'

'But our lunch,' she reminded him, she was very hungry. She remembered eating a good breakfast, but that now seemed a very long time ago.

'No time to stay for lunch,' Kester replied, as he jumped into the driving seat and took the reins from her. 'We will probably find them in Worcester if we press on, though Ambrose might have reached there before us. Don't go all missish on me, I am sure you are made of sterner stuff.'

'You are a brute,' she said to him. 'Even sensible girls get hungry, and you must be hungry yourself.'

'Never think of it,' he said. 'A good dinner at the end of the day . . . '

'And a bottle of wine, no doubt,' she remarked acidly.

'Wine? Yes, of course, but that

reminds me, have my brandy flask in my bag. Take a swig, it will soon restore your failing sensibilities.'

'Bah,' she said rudely, but reached for his bag and found the flask easily. She had more than a swig and felt better for the warmth and the comfort of the drink. She handed him the flask and she saw him take a long drink before driving out of the yard.'

After only a mile along the road, Delia regretted having brandy on an empty stomach. She felt light-headed and she also had hiccups.

'Kester,' she looked up at him. 'I've got hiccups.'

'Hold your breath.'

'I have tried that,' she said. 'It does not work.'

'It serves you right, you should not have had the brandy.'

'But you offered it to me,' she protested.

'I daresay I did, but you need not have had quite so much.'

Delia was feeling odd. 'I don't think I

like you very much, Kester.'

He did not take his eyes off the road. 'I daresay you don't, but I consider it a pity because I have taken a liking to you, Miss Stockdale.'

'Rubbish,' she retorted with another hiccup. 'You have only known me since breakfast time.'

'Did you have any breakfast?'

'Yes, I did,' she replied shortly and did not expect any sympathy.

She was right for he gave a grin. 'That is all right then, you can easily wait until dinner time.'

'Brute,' she said for the second time.

'Be quiet, we will soon be in Worcester.'

Delia did hold her breath then, and by the time they entered the city of Worcester, her hiccups had gone though she felt decidedly odd and regretted the brandy.

* ★ *

Worcester proved to be a nightmare. There were countless coaching houses and respectable taverns and Kester insisted on trying every one. His temper got shorter at each stop and when he came out of *The White Swan* to a miserably hungry Delia, it was not surprising that they had a quarrel.

'No sign of them,' he grunted as he sat beside her again. 'Devil take it, I'm damned if I know which is the more foolish of the two of them. My nephew for making such a wager or your stupid sister for going off with him.'

'She is not stupid,' Delia said hotly. 'She is a very young girl and she was misled by the impeccable manners of your Anthony when he came to call at The Furlongs. All girls of her age are romantic and she must have thought it a great adventure to run off to Gretna Green to be married.'

'Don't you dare jump to her defence. I have no doubt that she is a very pretty girl and that she put on her missish ways to ensnare Anthony.'

'It is your nephew who did the ensnaring, I might have you know, and poor little Katy walked right into the trap.' Delia was fast losing her temper with this gentleman; she considered him to be arrogant.

'Poor little Katy indeed! She knew just what she was doing, she had even packed her portmanteau and written a note to your mama. Then she had the gumption not to swallow the brandy you had so carefully prepared as soon as she had the suspicion that you had put laudanum into it. No, your sweet little sister is a young madam, there is no question about it. She is as much to blame as my disreputable nephew.'

'How dare you,' Delia was shouting. If I don't shout at him, I shall cry, she was telling herself. 'You are loathsome and I dislike you intensely.'

'I daresay you do, but I could soon change all that.'

Puzzled at his words and his tone, she looked up at him, but it was the wrong thing to do.

His lips were on hers in a tantalising sweet kiss. She felt strength and kindness from him and her exasperation vanished.

'Kester,' she breathed as she straightened up.

'I told you so,' he said and then he grinned at her. 'Delia Stockdale, you have never been kissed before. I can tell. What is your Ambrose about?'

Delia knew that she was still shaken by the kiss, but she replied robustly.

'Ambrose is a very respectable gentleman, he has often kissed me and always on the cheek very properly.'

Kester laughed. 'I am not surprised, my dear girl. Now I suggest we call a truce. We are at a pass in our hunt for the wretched pair and we have tried every single tavern in Worcester. I suggest that we stop here at *The White Swan*, have dinner and an early night and I don't mean together, my dear.'

'How dare you,' she flared again.

'I am sorry, it is a great joy to tease you and see the colour rise in your cheeks and the light of battle in your fine eyes.'

'Kester,' Delia said feebly, as she felt his fingers on her cheek, she could not fight him any more.

'Let me continue. We will have an early breakfast and then set off for Kidderminster, surely Anthony and Katy cannot have got farther than that.'

* * *

They did have a good dinner at *The White Swan*, and full of fine food and excellent wine, their tempers cooled and they found themselves chatting animatedly.

Delia was interested to hear about Pelham Grange and in return, told Kester of her plans for marrying Ambrose and settling at Ashleigh Court with the dowager. If he had a sceptical smile in his eyes, she chose to ignore it.

He escorted her to her bedroom door and said goodnight though not without a final attempt to secure her wrath.

'May I kiss you goodnight, Delia?'

'Of course not.' Delia had drunk a little too much wine.

But he had caught her arm and pulled her towards him and she was in his arms returning a kiss which was both quick and playful.

'Thank you, sweet Delia,' he whispered and walked off down the corridor to his own room.

Delia, confused, happy and slightly tipsy slept very well.

Next morning found them on the road very early. The horses were fresh, it was not far to Kidderminster and they had hopes of overtaking the runaways or at least catching up with an Ambrose who may have achieved more success than they had.

There was only one coaching house on that road and Delia was not surprised when Kester came back to the curricle shaking his head.

'Kidderminster next,' he said.

A few miles on and calamity struck.

It was Delia who spoke first.

'Kester, I do not want to worry you,

but is not one of your horses a little lame?'

'Lame? Nonsense, I have not noticed, but then I have been concentrating on all this traffic. I am astonished to find so many wagons on the road so early in the morning.'

'Perhaps it is market day in Kidderminster.'

'Nonsense,' he said again, the old terse manner returning.

But in a very few minutes, it became obvious that that horse was limping badly and Kester had to stop. He managed to take a quiet turning before jumping down to have a look.

'Curse it, he's cast a shoe,' he swore. 'Must have come loose on those rough lanes before we joined the turnpike road. Nothing for it, Delia, we will have to go back to Worcester and find a blacksmith.'

'Are we not nearer to Kidderminster?' she asked.

'No, we are not,' he answered her curtly. 'We are only a few miles out of

Worcester. This is becoming a deuced fruitless chase and I shall have to take my time with the horse in that state. Don't ever mention the names of Katy Stockdale and Anthony Mayfield to me again. I hope they are married by now and live to regret it.'

Delia thought it better to remain silent and they reached a blacksmith in Worcester without another word being said between them.

The blacksmith was busy and told them to come back in an hour.

'Now what do we do?' Kester asked grumpily as they left the smithy. 'I suppose we had better try and find a coffee house.'

Delia looked shocked. 'But, Kester, you cannot take a lady into a coffee house, you must know that.'

He glowered at her. 'I suppose you are right, what shall we do then?'

'It would be very nice if we could visit the cathedral. I have never seen it.'

'The cathedral? God preserve us, is that what Ambrose would have done?

How can you possibly love the man, Delia?'

Delia spoke in Ambrose's defence. 'He is a very good man and yes, he certainly would have wanted to visit the cathedral.'

Kester managed a grin. 'Off we go then, I cannot be outdone by the admirable Ambrose. Is there anything of particular interest in this cathedral of yours and how do you know about it in any case?'

'Papa has a lovely old book of all the cathedrals in England and there are many beautiful prints in it. I used to love to look at it. If I remember correctly, the crypt at Worcester is Norman and very interesting, and there are several notable tombs, particularly of King John.'

Delia sounded serious and very earnest, but Kester was smiling at her.

'An intelligent female, this I must see, and if there is no-one in this crypt of yours, then perhaps I will steal a kiss.'

'Kester,' Delia said, exasperated. But they set off walking through the streets of the city and were soon entering the red sandstone cathedral.

They walked quietly around, saw the tombs and monuments and went down the steep steps into the crypt. It was very dim, but they could see the rounded Norman arches which contrasted so startlingly with the tall and soaring perpendicular arches in the main cathedral.

Kester claimed his kiss and Delia did not protest, but told him it was disrespectful.

'I am disrespectful,' he replied light-heartedly. 'But I have enjoyed coming to this lovely place with you, Delia. Now we must resume our pursuit of the pair. I am beginning to regard it as pointless.'

★ ★ ★

The journey into Kidderminster passed in silence and without incident, but they entered the town with hope, neither of them knew the town, but it was not large and the main streets were easy to negotiate.

A call at *The Cross Keys* proved useless and when they drove into *The King's Head*, Delia began to feel despondent as she waited for Kester to appear with yet another report of failure.

When he came running out calling her name, she was astonished. She had never seen him so cheerful in all the few hours she had known him.

'Delia, come quickly, let me help you down. Our hunt is at an end.'

'But Katy? Is she here?' she asked as she climbed down from the curricle and took his arm into the tavern.

'No, she is not, but she was here yesterday and again this morning.'

The landlord was waiting for them and still had the note which Ambrose had written in his hand. He gave it to her.

'I understand that you are the young

lady's sister. She is quite safe now, Lord Coberley came for her yesterday. He said that she was his sister-in-law, so I imagine you to be Lady Coberley, I am pleased to welcome you and to tell you that he has taken her back to Gloucestershire.

Delia smiled her thanks to the landlord and then turned to Kester. He put his arm around her and she laid her head against his chest. If the landlord was astonished at the ways of the gentry, he showed nothing in his expression.

'Thank God, Kester,' Delia said. 'Dear Ambrose, Katy will be safely at home by now, what a lot of trouble she has caused us these past two days.'

They thanked the landlord and he arranged an early luncheon for them. It was only just after twelve o'clock when they set off for Prestbury. Kester assured Delia that if they did not have to stop for anything then they would be home before dark.

'I think I would like to stop

somewhere for dinner, Kester, now that we know that Katy is safe.'

'Very well, my dear,' he said meekly and she looked at him suspiciously, but he led her out of *The King's Arms* quite cheerfully.

* * *

Their journey home went smoothly. They stopped for their dinner at *The Duke Of Buckingham* and it was mid-evening when they arrived at The Furlongs.

Delia insisted that Kester came into the house to make sure that Katy was really there. He did so reluctantly.

They found a subdued Katy with her mother in the drawing-room and Delia made the introductions.

'Kester, this is my sister, Katy, who has caused all this trouble. Katy, this is Kester Mayfield who is uncle to your Anthony . . . '

'He is not my Anthony any more,' Katy said with a scowl. 'He completely deceived me and I had to run away from him. Now I have discovered that he did it all for a wager, I never wish to hear his name mentioned again.'

Then she suddenly found her manners. 'Mr Mayfield . . . Kester, Anthony always calls you . . . I must thank you very much for coming after me and for taking Delia with you. But dear Ambrose got to Kidderminster first and has brought me home. I am quite in disgrace with Mama and Papa.'

She smiled up at him and Kester could see why his nephew had been so taken with her, but how very different from Delia she is, he was thinking, and he turned to Katy's sister.

''All's well that ends well' as they say. Delia, come and see me off. There is something I wish to say to you.' He made a bow to them all and guided Delia to the door.

Delia was puzzled by his request. She was also very tired. She felt that all she wanted to do was to give Katy a good shake and then seek the comfort of her own bed.

She stood at the front porch with Kester and Delia knew that she must thank him for his efforts on behalf of Katy. She spoke very formally.

'Kester, I must offer you my thanks for all you have done on Katy's behalf. I do not suppose that we shall meet again and I want you to know that we are all very grateful to you.'

He laughed then and Delia looked put out.

'Why are you laughing at me?' she demanded.

'You are so formal and correct, my love, and all I want to do is to take you in my arms, tell you that I have fallen in love with you and that I would like to ask you if you would kindly marry me.'

8

The front of The Furlongs had just caught the last rays of the setting sun and in the mellow light, Delia looked at Kester in astonishment.

His expression was serious, his eyes kindly and loving.

'What are you saying, Kester?'

'I'm asking you to marry me, Delia. I love you, I have only known you for two days, but I know I love you. Indeed, I think I fell in love with you the moment you opened this very door thinking that I was Ambrose.'

This remark brought Delia to her senses.

'By why do you say such things? You know very well that I am to marry Ambrose in just a few weeks time. You are talking nonsense.'

'Is it nonsense to tell a young lady that you love her?'

Delia was confused, her feelings mixed, her understanding seemed to have fled in her tiredness.

'I am sorry, Kester, but you must know what my answer has to be. I am engaged to marry Ambrose.'

'But you do not love him.'

Delia knew that she did not love Ambrose, she knew that her feelings for him were very lukewarm, but nevertheless she had agreed to marry him.

'I have known forever that I would marry him, he is a very kind person as you will have realised today.'

'I have no doubt that he is kind,' he replied rather abruptly, 'but is kindness enough?'

'It is enough for me,' Delia's reply sounded feeble.

'You are a fool,' he said tersely and without another word, he took her in his arms and kissed her. Delia was tired, but she longed for Kester's kiss and did not deny him.

Then suddenly she was free, and he was running down the steps to his curricle, he jumped up and was away.

'Now tell me that you love Ambrose,' he called out.

Delia watched as the curricle disappeared down the drive. I have refused the only man I shall ever love, she told herself and almost wept. But I cannot let Ambrose down, it was always agreed that I would marry him and he has been so good to us.

Delia had no idea of Ambrose's change of heart and she turned to go back into the house with a feeling of loss. She had waited for love and now she had turned it down.

★　★　★

After Katy's escapade, no more was to be heard of Anthony Mayfield, neither did Mr Kester Mayfield call at The Furlongs again.

Delia had moments of deep regret, of a real sadness, but the preparations were going ahead and Ambrose visited every day.

It was after one of these visits that Delia was to have a slight spat with Katy who had been very quiet and subdued since the affair of Anthony Mayfield as they now called it.

Delia had felt out of sympathy with Ambrose that day. He had been full of plans to take her on the continent for their honeymoon, but Delia was reluctant to commit herself to days spent in the carriage with Ambrose reading from the guide book to her at each town they passed through.

That Ambrose was equally reluctant to spend this kind of holiday with his bride was completely unknown to Delia. He thought that it was the correct thing to do for a gentleman of his standing and made the plans accordingly, without asking Delia what she would like to do.

There was little rapport between them and Katy was quick to notice it and then remark upon it.

'Why are you so unenthusiastic when Ambrose talks about your honeymoon,

Delia? I cannot but notice it.'

'It is what Ambrose wants to do, Katy, and that is good enough for me,' was Delia's snappish reply.

'How do you know if it is what he wants to do if you never talk about it between yourselves?'

Delia was incensed. 'And how do you know what we talk about in private, young miss?'

'I don't, but I can guess. I love Ambrose, as a brother of course, and I know what he likes and I am sure that he does not want a journey all through France and Italy with only you for company.'

'Katy,' said an outraged Delia. 'You are being impertinent. What goes on between Ambrose and myself is our own private affair and I do not need you to take me to task over it.'

'I am sorry, Delia, but I do think that Ambrose seems troubled and it upsets me. He was very good to me when he found me in Kidderminster with Jacob the tramp, he was so pleased to have seen me and was very polite to Jacob.'

The story of Katy's escape from the arms of Anthony Mayfield had been told many times, but this was the first time that Delia had heard Ambrose praised for his part in it all.

'Ambrose behaved very correctly,' Katy added.

'I would expect him to do so and I will not tolerate any criticism of his plans for our honeymoon, young lady . . . now what is it?' She noticed a dark look come into Katy's face.

'You do not love him,' her sister muttered, and Katy ran from the room.

What was all that about, Delia asked herself as Katy disappeared. Surely the child is never fancying herself in love with Ambrose because he rescued her from Anthony's clutches? She sighed. Sometimes I wonder if we can possibly be sisters, she thought sadly.

Ambrose arrived at The Furlongs later in the day when Delia was already out riding. It had always been their practice to ride together, but he had not appeared that day and she decided to ride out on her own.

She felt restless and with an uneasy lowering of spirits. There had been no reason to suppose that she would ever see Kester Mayfield again after she had turned him down, but she often found herself thinking of him.

Sir John Mayfield had paid her father a courtesy visit to apologise for Anthony's behaviour and told him that the episode seemed to have shaken his son as he had settled well into this position in Gloucester.

There were only two or three weeks to go to her marriage to Ambrose. All the arrangements had been made and the waiting seemed endless.

So it was that she enjoyed the gallop on Cleeve Common and handing her horse over at the stables, she started to walk towards the house. Then she paused as she thought she could see figures in the shrubbery.

She stopped. It was undoubtedly Ambrose, but who was it with him?

They seemed to be talking earnestly. Not feeling in the least guilty, she crept silently nearer until she was close enough to see that it was Katy who was with Ambrose. Not only that, they were holding hands.

She stayed still and watched, trying to imagine what they were saying. Then she held her breath as she saw Katy taken close into Ambrose's arms and kissed passionately. His arms were clinging round her neck and to Delia's utmost astonishment, she saw Ambrose kiss the girl's shoulders, then let his lips move to the low neck of Katy's fashionable sprig muslin.

They loved each other, Delia gasped. She did not know if she had said the words out loud or not, but it did not matter for she ran quickly forward into the shrubbery, calling their names.

'Katy! Ambrose!'

The pair jumped apart, but Ambrose held on to Katy's hand.

'Delia,' he said. 'I apologise profoundly, but Katy and I love each other very much. I will be honest and tell you now that I have always loved Katy, but she was such a young little thing, and a marriage between you and myself had always been planned. Will you forgive us?'

Delia walked up to them. There seemed to be a song of joy in her heart.

She took Katy's hand and kissed her.

'I think I guessed,' she said, 'and I will gladly cry off, Ambrose. But the plans we have made for the wedding, what shall we do?'

Katy was suddenly excited and gave Delia a kiss.

'You are a darling sister and I am sorry if I have taken Ambrose from you, but I know you did not love him as I did. It was strange, Delia, although I loved him, he was always too old and too important for me, then suddenly, I seemed to grow up and I realised he loved me, too.' She stopped, kissed them both, then looked up at Ambrose.

'Are you going to ask me to marry you, Ambrose or do you have to ask Papa first?'

He smiled. 'I will ask your father, my dear, but I hope you will not refuse me.'

'Oh, I do say yes and we could have the same date for the wedding, could we not? It would only mean changing the invitations, they have not been sent out yet.'

Delia laughed then. 'Stop, Katy, stop. There is no reason why you should not be married on that same day, but you should consult Ambrose.'

'Ambrose will do whatever I want, won't you?' she smiled up at him and Delia was horrified at her forward behaviour. Then she heard his words.

'Of course, my little love, whatever you wish.'

They all went back into the house together to make the change of plans known to Sir James and Lady Patricia. Katy's mother did not seem in the least surprised, though she did question her young daughter on her habit of falling in and out of love. What about Anthony, she asked?

'Anthony!' Katy exclaimed. 'I was

just a foolish and romantic girl and did not know what true love is. It is all different with Ambrose.'

Delia met her mother's eyes and they smiled. It was only a few weeks ago, they seemed to be telling each other. But Lady Patricia's main concern seemed to be about the wedding gown.

'Katy, however can we get you a gown made in time? Delia's would never fit you.'

Nothing would daunt Katy that day. 'We will have a white overdress made for my come-out gown, that will do perfectly well. Oh, and Ambrose, can we go to Scotland for the honeymoon, I would love that and I am sure you did not want to go to France and Italy as you told Delia. Mama, Delia, is it not very exciting?'

★ ★ ★

At Pelham Grange at this time, was to be found a rather sober Kester Mayfield. He worked hard about the estate, he went riding, he even travelled over the Gloucester to see if his young nephew was settled.

He found Anthony quite unrepentant, but surprisingly liking his work and enjoying his freedom of being a young man about town again.

And Kester thought a lot about Delia. He had been quite honest when he had told her that he loved her and it had only taken forty-eight hours in her company to realise that she was a girl of spirit and not one of the silly young misses he had encountered at the Cheltenham Assembly Rooms in his younger days.

That she should prefer the staid Lord Coberley to himself, he found a very hard fact to swallow. I suppose we will be receiving an invitation to the wedding, he would think somewhat sorrowfully, though he did remember that Delia had said that it would be a quiet affair.

It was his custom to talk over the affairs of the estate with his brother in the first hour after breakfast each day. So it was that one morning in late June, he went into Sir John's library to find him frowning over a card, perhaps an invitation, which he had just received.

'Good morning, Kester. I thought you told me that Viscount Coberley of Ashleigh Court was to marry the eldest Stockdale girl, Delia I think you said her name was.

'Yes, Delia is to marry Ambrose, I believe it to be an old family arrangement and not an affair of the heart. Why do you ask?'

Sir John frowned. 'We have received an invitation to the wedding ... Miss Katherine Stockdale, youngest daughter of Sir James and Lady Patricia Stockdale to Ambrose Staynford, Viscount Coberley of Ashleigh Court on the ...

He snatched the card from his brother's hand and read the words for himself.

'It is true. What the devil made her change her mind? And Ambrose and

Katy, it can't be true. Congratulate me, John.'

Sir John Mayfield looked bemused. 'You are talking nonsense, Kester. Wait, wait, don't rush off without giving me an explanation.'

'I asked Delia to marry me and she refused. I love the girl, John and you will love her, too. She was determined on marrying Ambrose because the family has arranged it years ago, but I knew it was me she loved. I knew it.'

Kester rode quickly back to Fulwood House for the curricle and was off on the Cheltenham road in a flash.

At The Furlongs, he was to be disappointed. Katy and her mother were visiting at Ashleigh Court, Delia had gone riding and only Sir James was at home.

Kester was welcomed into the library and he told Delia's father of his mission.

'You want to marry, Delia? Thank heaven, I believe her to be mooning after you ever since the affair of your nephew. You know about Ambrose and little Katy, I suppose? I am not sure that I approve. Delia would have suited him far better, but it seems that he and Katy love each other.

'He is twelve years older than she is, but my wife and I believe that it might be a good thing for her. We have spoilt the little minx, running off with Anthony Mayfield, indeed, of course he is your nephew. That scandal seems to have been forgotten, thank goodness, and now it is Katy who is to marry Ambrose. You don't need to ask my permission to address Delia, she is out riding. Will you wait for her to come home or will you go after her? I expect she is up on Cleeve Common somewhere.'

'I am in my curricle,' said Kester impatiently.

'No matter, tell the stable boy to saddle my hunter, Solomon, for you. He is good-tempered enough and he is a flyer so will get you up to the common in no time at all. And make sure that you persuade Delia to accept your proposal.'

Kester grinned. 'I will,' he said and was gone.

At the common he found no sign of Delia. He went almost as far as the ancient earthworks at Belas Knap, he came back and rode round Cleeve Cloud as the lower part of the common was called. But still he did not spot Delia and his patience was being tested.

I will have to return to The Furlongs and see if she is at home. What a way to go wooing.

He left Solomon at the stables and went to talk to Sir James. He was met on his way to the house by Katy and her mother. They were just returned from Ashleigh Court and were getting out of the carriage.

Katy came flying up to him in excitement. 'Kester, have you received the invitation? Is it not all very exciting? We have not seen you. I hope you will congratulate us, we are very happy.'

'I offer my felicitations, Katy, and I

trust that you and Ambrose will be very happy. Do you know where Delia is? I wish to see her.'

Katy made a face. 'I hope you will cheer her up then, she has had a fit of the dismals, I think it is because I am so excited that it will soon be my wedding to my dear Ambrose. I thought that Delia had gone riding up on the common.'

'Her horse is back in the stables.'

'Then you are sure to find her in the summer house, she usually takes a book out there after she has been riding.'

He found the summer house easily and in it was Delia, quietly reading. He thought that she looked lovely in pale blue muslin with an unusually high neck and buttons to the waist.

Delia had indeed been out of sorts since the engagement of Katy and Ambrose had been celebrated. Knowing that she loved Kester, she was miserable at having refused his offer though she had no alternative at the time. She felt an aching disappointment that he had not visited them again.

When she glanced up from her book and saw him standing there in the entrance to the summer house, her heart gave a bound.

'Kester,' she cried out.

'Delia, I have found you at last. I hope you enjoyed your gallop.'

She looked puzzled. 'I did not ride this morning. It was overcast so I decided to wait until this afternoon. I brought my book to the summer house instead . . . why, what is it, Kester?'

He had sat down beside her and taken her by the shoulders, turning her to face him.

'Are you telling me that you have not been riding on Cleeve Common this morning?'

'Yes . . . no, I mean I have not. Does it matter? Kester . . . ' she cried out as he took her in his arms.

'I have ridden three times round the common looking for you, I have been as far as Belas Knap, I have searched for you on Cleeve Cloud and you are telling me that you have been sitting here all this time?'

'Yes, that is right . . . Kester, what are you doing?'

His fingers were on the buttons of her blue dress. 'I am determined to have a glimpse of the you that is hidden under your dress. I want to kiss you all over. Keep still.'

And Delia was mesmerised into stillness by his lips on her breast, her throat and then on her lips in a long kiss. She raised her arms around his neck and crept closer to him; she was where she longed to be.

'You didn't come to see me,' she murmured.

'I should think not! How could I come to see you when you were intent on marrying Ambrose.' He put her away from him, loving the disorder of her dress and the pretty flush on her cheeks.

'I thought you might have heard that Katy was going to marry him.'

'I did not. Give me another kiss . . . I

did not know until this very morning when we received the invitation to *Katy's* wedding to Ambrose. Not yours, but Katy's. What does it all mean?'

She started to do up the buttons of her dress, but his lips stopped her and she gave a deep breath of pleasure.

'I found Katy and Ambrose kissing, they were just over there in the shrubbery, so I cried off. They are so happy and I cannot quite believe it for it seems the most unlikely match. She is so much younger than he is.'

'I think your Katy received a fright when she ran off with Anthony, I have been to see him, by the way, and Ambrose became not only her hero, but her love. And it seemed obvious to me that Ambrose loved Katy the way he went racing after her. I hope they will be very happy. And that is enough about them, what about us?'

'What about us?' Delia asked.

'I told you I loved you, I asked you to marry me and you turned me down. I have missed you abominably these past weeks and I still love you so I will ask you again. Have you forgotten about Ambrose? Do you love me and will you please marry me?'

She smiled and put a finger on his lips.

'I never did love Ambrose, I know now that I was waiting for love all that time and then you came. So the answer is yes to both your questions.'

'Say it then.'

She laughed and the laugh was a merry one.

'I love you, Kester Mayfield, and I will be pleased to accept your offer of marriage.'

THE END

BELLE OF THE BALL

Anne Holman

When merchandise is stolen from the shop where Isabel Hindley works, she and the other shop assistants are under suspicion. So when Lady Yettington is observed going out of the shop without paying for goods, Isabel accuses her ladyship of theft, making her nephew, Charles Yettington, furious. But things are more complicated when Lady Yettington is put under surveillance, and more merchandise goes missing. Isabel and Charles plan to find out who is responsible.

THE KINDLY LIGHT

Valerie Holmes

Annie Darton's life was happiness itself, living with her father, the lighthouse keeper of Gannet Rock, until an accident changed their lives forever. Forced to move, Annie's path crosses with the attractive stranger, Zachariah Rudd. Shrouded in mystcry, undoubtedly hiding something, he becomes steadily more involved in Annie's life, especially when the new lighthouse keeper is murdered. Annie finds herself drawn into the mysteries around her. Only by resolving the past can she look to the future, whatever the cost!

LOVE AND WAR

Joyce Johnson

Alison Dowland is about to marry her childhood sweetheart, Joe, when his regiment is recalled to battle, and American soldiers descend on the tiny Cornish harbour of Porthallack to prepare for the D-day landings. Excitement is high as the villagers prepare to welcome their allies, but to her dismay, Alison falls in love with American Chuck Bartlett. Amidst an agonising personal decision, she is also caught up in espionage, endangering herself and her sister.

OPPOSITES ATTRACT

Chrissie Loveday

Jeb Marlow was not happy to trust his life to the young pilot who was to fly him through a New Zealand mountain range in poor weather. What was more, the pilot was a girl. Though they were attracted, Jacquetta soon realised they lived in different worlds; he had a champagne lifestyle, dashing around the world, and she helped run an isolated fruit farm in New Zealand. Could they ever have any sort of relationship or would their differences always come between them?